MW01126062

FURY

FORSAKEN MERCENARY BOOK THREE

JONATHAN YANEZ

CONTENTS

BOOKS IN THE FORSAKEN MERCENARY
UNIVERSE

2. Cassie

STAY INFORMED

Get A Free Book by visiting Jonathan Yanez' website. You can email me at jonathan.alan.yanez@gmail.com or find me on Amazon, and Instagram (@author_jonathan_yanez). I also created a special Facebook group called "Jonathan's Reading Wolves" specifically for readers, where I show new cover art, do giveaways, and run contests. Please check it out and join whenever you get the chance!

For updates about new releases, as well as exclusive promotions, visit my website and sign up for the VIP mailing list. Head there now to receive free stories.

www.jonathan-yanez.com

Enjoying the series? Help others discover *Forsaken Mercenary* by sharing with a friend.

ONE

TRUE TO HIS WORD, Preacher had transportation for us from Elysium to the far side of Mars in a few hours' time. The plan was to get as close as we could via air travel. We'd go in the rest of the way on foot.

Preacher piloted a small two-person craft he called a Raptor as we sped through the midday air toward the unknown. If I wasn't so dead sure that I could trust Preacher, I wouldn't have tried any of this. The bond we shared was something I couldn't put my finger on.

It was the same kind of feeling when I saw Wesley Cage, but even stronger. This was a man I had bonded with through spilling the blood of our enemies and bleeding together.

"You gonna tell me about that AI you have

connected to your head or just keep it a secret for now?" Preacher asked after a few hours in silence.

We had left the airspace over the city. Below us lay nothing except open land made up of red sand dunes and mountain ranges. Occasional valleys cut through the terrain, but never water.

"X, want to introduce yourself?" I asked.

"Hello," X said to Preacher. "My designation is quite a bit longer, but we have decided to go with X for now."

"X, I heard Immortal Corp was making these assistants for operatives in the field," Preacher pointed out. "I didn't know they were operational yet."

"Wesley Cage." I said the name as if that were answer enough.

"Cage." Preacher repeated the name. "He's a good man. I'm not sure you remember that, but he's one of the few good ones. Better even than you or me."

"He was the one that recruited us?" I asked.

"Yep, found the seven of us not due to our intelligence, physical prowess, or anything else we possessed, short of our spirit to go on," Preacher said with a slight tilt of his chin. "He brought us together. Oversaw our training and acted as a handler to send us out on missions."

"If you don't mind me asking, why are you so—so—"

"Old?" Preacher looked over at me with a twinkle in his one good eye.

"I was going to say 'seasoned,'" I said with a grin. "But yeah, let's go with old."

"The Pack Protocol needed a leader in the field," Preacher explained. "Cage decided it would be easier if there were someone older to command respect. I got the job. I was a teacher before I joined the Pack, believe it or not."

I couldn't help but laugh.

"Sorry, sorry." I cleared my throat. "I just can't imagine you as a teacher. What did you teach?"

"History," Preacher said. "Never thought I'd be writing it. Or the one protecting it from being erased."

The cabin grew silent.

"How long have—they been watching us?" I asked, not able to bring myself to say the word 'alien.' "How do you know they're hostile?"

"We suspect it's been years," Preacher said, staring out the front of the craft. "They've been preparing and planning. They're patient. We know they're hostile because they've abducted humans over the years, experimenting on them, torturing them. The equipment they're bringing in isn't for a social hour either. We can say that for sure."

"How has the population not noticed an alien presence on the opposite side of the planet?" I asked, still trying to wrap my mind around it. "How can this not be mainstream news?"

"I think you're giving people too much credit," Preacher said. "Outside of Elysium, there are only two other major cities on Mars. The rest are smaller wealthy communities. Not even a quarter of Mars has been colonized. We're working with a population here that can't number more than a few million. You think they're interested in exploring the deserted parts of Mars or more willing to sit in their nice couches watching the latest holo show and sipping their designer caf drinks?"

Preacher didn't have to say more. He drove his point home with every word that left his mouth.

"There's a couple meal bars in the back and some water," Preacher said. "You should grab some shuteye if you can. We still have about a day of travel."

"I'll do that, but I still feel like I have a million questions to ask you outside of this coming alien invasion. I can't even believe I'm saying that right now," I said. "I want to know everything you do about

Immortal Corp, the Pack, and our time training together."

Preacher took the next few hours hitting all the key points, some of which I knew. Other stories were completely foreign to me.

It seemed the two members of the Pack I hadn't met yet, Jax and Angel, were still active assets employed by Immortal Corp, like Echo and Preacher. When we were first recruited, we spent five years training in everything from hand-to-hand combat to weapons; bladed, blunt, and firearms.

The genetic experimentation we went through was also conducted during this time. In those years, we grew as not just a pack but a family. In the following years, we went on dozens of missions with a one hundred percent success rate.

Amber and I always had eyes for each other. A few years in, we started dating. A few years later, we got engaged.

"I'd be on my way out like Sam, maybe even working a way to try and bring Immortal Corp under some kind of accountability, but not now," Preacher said, finishing his story. "Not with what we know now about the alien invasion. I can't. Immortal Corp is the only power in the galaxy that's willing to take a stand. They're humanity's best bet to surviving any of this."

We continued talking for hours about training and missions we went on. More and more memories that felt like dreams swam to the surface. The closest I could get to putting what I felt into words was waking and trying to recall a dream I just had. A dream that was just out of reach.

The day began to shift to night. We ate the tasteless meal bars and water. The more I got to know about Preacher, the more I knew my feeling of trust was well-founded. He was just a guy trying to do the right thing with what he was given.

When night came, I didn't try to fight sleep. I found a place to lie down and I passed out hard. If I had known what was waiting for me when I awoke, I would have had Preacher turn the craft around.

I wasn't sure how long I'd slept. I knew it was through the night because the sun was already coming up over the Martian horizon. The Raptor was just large enough for me to lie down behind the pilot's and co-pilot's seats. The hard floor wasn't exactly comfortable, but I'd been through a lot of uncomfortable situations.

"There he is," Preacher said, twisting in his seat to look at me. "I was going to wake you up, but you were snoring like some kind of hibernating animal, so I let you be. I saw a bear once in a zoo on Mars. You sounded a lot like him."

"Yeah, I slept surprisingly well," I said, stretching as much as the inside of the Raptor would allow. I leaned down to look out the front window of the craft. "Where are we now?"

The landscape looked exactly the same to me as everything else. Red, lots of red sand, a few mountains in the distance, and more red sand.

"Close," Preacher said. "We're getting close. We'll set down soon and go the rest of the way on foot."

I was about to ask another question, when the radio crackled to life.

As soon as the strange noise infiltrated the Raptor, it was gone again. It happened so fast, I had to take a seat next to Preacher and look over to make sure I hadn't just made it up.

"No," Preacher said with a grim look of determination on his face. "No such luck, *mijo*. I heard it too."

"It sounded like a click, or a tick from someone's throat?" I asked, trying to put words to the sound I had just heard. "Is that them?"

"We think so," Preacher answered. "As you can expect, they're more advanced than we are. They have cloaking technology for both their physical presence and their digital presence. Every once in a while, we get lucky and pick up a short burst of a transmission like you heard, but that's it."

I sat quietly in my seat.

What have I gotten myself into? I thought to myself. *The vanguard in an intergalactic war?*

"So what's the plan?" I asked, trying to bring some kind of order to this insane situation. "We go spy on them and then what? We gather evidence so that the Galactic Government can't ignore us and have to send in the Praetorian Militia?"

"We go in and gather intel, but no matter how much evidence we get, the Galactic Government will turn a blind eye," Preacher said with disgust. "They'll pass it off as a hoax or something worse. They'll bury it to avoid mass panic. The GG is all about order. Do you think they'll see an alien invasion as orderly?"

"That's insane," I said, not trying to hide the frustration in my voice. "They have to listen to us. I mean, with the right evidence, how could they not? We can take pictures, radio samples, even—"

I stopped myself before I finished my thought.

"What?" Preacher asked.

"What if we captured one?" I asked. "They would have to believe us then."

Preacher turned his one good eye at me as if I had gone clinically insane.

"X, he always like this?" Preacher asked.

"I'm afraid, yes, at least most of the time," X answered. "Does his current desire for havoc match his previous character? I mean, when he was training and going on missions with you?"

"Oh yeah," Preacher affirmed like I wasn't even in the Raptor with them. "He was the real shoot first ask questions later kind of deal."

"Hey," I interjected, interrupting the two "I'm right here. I can hear everything you're saying."

"He took on an entire army along with Sam," X answered. "It was his idea."

"Doesn't surprise me in the slightest." Preacher chuckled. "Once we went on a mission where a crazed scientist was mutating animals. This son of a gun stares down a mutated lion like he's looking at himself in a mirror. The crazy thing is that it worked. That chimera hybrid wanted no part of him."

"Still right here," I said despite myself. In all honesty, I wanted to know about this mission with the chimera.

"So what's your plan?" Preacher asked, changing the subject from mutated chimera beasts. "We capture an alien, stroll into the GG's capitol building, demand an audience, and drop an alien carcass at the feet of our esteemed leader?"

"Something like that." I shrugged. "What else you got? We take on the alien invasion alone?"

"As much as I believe in you and me, *mijo*, we wouldn't stand a chance," Preacher said. His tone turned from jovial to hard once more. "Not against them."

The cabin quieted.

Preacher dwelled on the future in silence. I took a moment to look down at the Raptor's control panel. A screen showed a 3D image of the surrounding landscape.

As far as I could tell, there was nothing. Nothing but kilometers of sand and more sand. The far side of Mars didn't look like much, if Preacher was right, it held a terrible secret.

"We're here," Preacher said, taking control of the Raptor from the automatic drive feature and setting us down behind a high sand dune. "We'll need to trek in a few—"

The radio crackled again, this time longer and more distinct, guttural ticks that came in sporadic intervals. I wasn't sure I could make the same noises if I wanted to.

A wave of goosebumps crossed my skin as the transmission died once again.

"You good?" Preacher asked. "I remember how I felt when I heard them for the first time. It's horrifying, dreadful, amazing, and shocking all at once."

"I'm good," I confirmed, rising from my seat. "Let's go hunt some aliens."

TWO

FOR ITS SIZE, the Raptor held a surprising amount of gear. Overhead compartments set into each side of the Raptor carried water, food, supplies, and survival equipment to see us through the excursion.

A hover bot assured that we wouldn't have to carry any of it. The bot was a flat piece of steel that hovered just above the ground. Preacher stacked and secured our equipment on the bot then set it to follow him at a few meters' distance.

I checked my MK II, my knife, and axe.

Preacher eyed the bladed weapon on my belt.

"You still prefer the old school means of fighting," Preacher observed, jerking his chin to the knife and axe. He patted the hilt of the katana over his shoulder. "I guess I can't blame you."

Once we were out of the Raptor, Preacher pressed a series of buttons on his left vambrace. I didn't notice the piece of tech he wore before. It was a dull metal grey with an interface screen set on the top of his forearm.

One minute, the Raptor was right in front of us, the next, it was gone, completely cloaked from any prying eye, human or other.

I knew cloaking technology existed but had yet to experience it firsthand.

"Come on, we have a few hours to go yet," Preacher said, waving me forward.

We headed into the vast Martian desert with the hover bot in tow.

Preacher gave me a poncho with a deep hood that protected me from the hot sun while blending me in with the landscape. He wore one himself. The color of the fabric was perfectly suited to make us nearly invisible to the naked eye.

Preacher even put one on the hover bot. It seemed whatever tech cloaked the Raptor had not yet been modified to cloak us or the small bot.

We walked in silence as the day's rays beat down on us. Soon a new mountain range to the north touched the sky in front of us.

"There it is." Preacher nodded toward the mountain. "That's where they've touched down and made their staging area. There's a system of caves that goes down into the ground. We suspect they're using that as well as a forward base we can't see in front of the mountain range. They have it cloaked."

I blinked a few times, trying to make out any kind of shimmer or ripple that would give away a cloaked base in front of the mountain.

Nothing.

"X," I asked as Preacher and I took a knee behind a low dune. "Do you have anything that would allow us to see the cloaking shield?"

"I'm not positive anything I have will help," X mused out loud. "We can't be sure what kind of technology we're dealing with here. Let me run through a few options. Keep your eyes open and trained on where we think the cloak is in front of you."

I obeyed. What I saw next was a series of images in front of my eyes as X tried different viewing options. She zoomed in, tried night visions, then a dozen options I didn't have names for. The view in front of me changed faster and faster from greens to blues and whites and black. I had to blink a few times. The colors were changing so fast, I thought I was going to have a seizure or worse.

The beginnings of a headache were upon me. I was

about to ask X for a break, when she stopped. A massive dome twice the size of the mountain behind it stood in front of me.

My jaw worked up and down, but I wasn't sure what to say. The dome had to be the size of a small city, and shone red, orange, and yellow.

"What do you see?" Preacher whispered excitedly. "What is it?"

"The cloaked base in front of the mountain is larger than the mountain itself," I managed to get out. "I wish you could take a look at this. X, how are we seeing this?"

"Infrared," X answered. "The dome they're using to conceal themselves has a slight heat signature I'm able to magnify. It would be invisible to the naked eye or any other infrared tech available. I have the infrared enhanced by over one hundred percent at the moment."

I tried to swallow, but there was no spit in my mouth. My mind was having a hard time processing the truth behind what I was seeing. The dome could easily fit thousands of human soldiers. I could only guess that thousands of aliens waited within.

Preacher had told me what we were up against. Still, it was one thing to talk about the impossible and something entirely different to see it in front of you.

"Any sign of movement within?" Preacher asked. "Can you see anything other than the dome?"

"Nothing," I told him. "The dome is a throbbing mix of orange, red, and yellows. It goes up at least a hundred stories into the sky. The base has to be a few kilometers wide."

"How are we going to get in?" Preacher asked out loud. "We'll have to wait for night, but we have no way of knowing if the cloak is something we can pass through. I—"

Preacher stopped mid-sentence. His hand reached for the hilt of his blade. Something invisible collided with the side of his jaw, sending him crumpling to the ground.

I reached for my knife and blade. I didn't trust that my MK II wouldn't make enough noise to bring the entire alien dome down on us.

While I withdrew my weapons, X was just as fast at zeroing in on our enemy using her magnified infrared trick. I saw the form too late. A series of blows that landed on my face and torso paralyzed my body as my mind tried to make sense of the macabre figure laying into me.

The figure was slightly taller than me with four arms and two legs. Its head was roughly the same size and shape as my own, as was the torso. Anything more specific would have to wait to be seen. The cloaking device the alien wore made it impossible for me to make out any details.

With four arms and the element of surprise, I was on my knees in seconds. Blood dripped from my mouth and a cut over my left eye. As each blow landed, my body exploded in a wave of new pain.

I was used to fighting people I could see. People who had two arms not four.

On my knees, weapons still in hand, I struggled to rise.

"He's striking in the same series of blows," X said in a rush of words. "Right left, from the upper arms, left right from the lower arms."

I didn't have time to say thank you before the alien was at it again. I pushed myself to my feet as the alien followed the pattern X laid out for me. It came at me with a right fist that I sank my knife into.

A screech of pain exploded from the previously silent alien's throat. This wasn't a click or a tick, not even a howl. It was a screech like some kind of bird.

The alien took a moment to recover, trying to regain its plan of attack. I had been in enough fights to know this was my moment of opportunity.

I ripped the blade free from its hand and slammed my axe into its chest. Unlucky for me, the alien wore some kind of heavy armor that turned my blade. Lucky for me, the blade did manage to strike and hamper its cloaking device.

The reddish, orange, and yellow outline I had been fighting shimmered and sparkled. The cloak dissipated altogether, showing something I never could have imagined.

The alien was armored with a series of dark metal plates over most of its body. The sections that were not armored, like its hands and feet, were a pale greyish color. Two fingers and a thumb on each hand made for perfect weapons of blunt damage.

Its face was impossible to see past a steel-colored helmet that encompassed its entire head. The helmet did have a series of six red lights that looked like they were in the right position to be eyes.

That was all I had time to see.

The alien recovered, grabbing some kind of crude weapon from its back with one of its uninjured arms while the other two arms pressed the attack.

The initial shock of the ambush had worn off enough for me to recover and form an attack of my own. I batted away one arm that reached for my hand that held the knife. I slammed the axe head into the next reaching arm.

The alien screeched in pain once more. It swiped

down with the arm that had reached behind its back, the weapon now in hand. The slice took a chunk of my right shoulder with it. The blow was expertly placed just outside where the lightweight vest I wore came to an end.

White-hot pain exploded in my shoulder.

I gritted my teeth, taking a step away from my opponent and trying to create distance while coming up with a plan to combat this thing.

The alien pressed the attack, leaping forward with as much strength as a Cyber Hunter. I blocked the overhead blow with both my axe and knife. The strength this alien possessed was horrifying. My arms trembled as the axe and knife grated against the alien weapon.

The weapon was some kind of sword with a serrated edge on one side and a sharp blade on the other.

The alien used its two good arms to bear down on the hilt, forcing the blade toward my head. To create more distance, I went down to a knee. My arms were about to go out. The alien sword inched closer to my face and head.

The alien leaned in, sure of its victory.

A red blade punctured its chest out of nowhere. From my vantage point, I couldn't see Preacher behind the alien. All I saw was the bright humming red blade being forced up through the creature's sternum, its skull, and out the top end.

The alien's body quivered as black blood dowsed both the red sand and me.

Preacher stood behind the alien as it fell. He looked ready to skewer the creature again if the need called. Lucky for us, there was no need.

"Thanks," I managed after a long lungful of air.

"We should've known they'd have scouts," Preacher said, not even looking at me. His eyes were glued to the alien corpse at our feet.

I stood up, studying the creature. I had time now to take in all the details I missed before. It was long limbed and bony. The helmet it wore was severed in two, thanks to Preacher. I had my first look at its face. Or at least two halves of its face. I was right. Six eyes —three on each side—looked at me unseeing. Its mouth was similar to our own, but the nose was more like two holes. No ears that I could see, or hear

"We need to get out of here," Preacher said. "This is proof enough. We need to go befo—"

Glimmering orange and red all around sent warnings off in my mind. We weren't alone.

"Preacher," I interrupted, putting my back to his. "We've got more company."

THREE

HE TOOK MY MEANING.

We stood quiet, back to back as the aliens turned off their cloaking devices. One by one, they appeared all around us. There had to be dozens of the creatures. They varied slightly in height and build, but it was clear they were all the same species.

Unlike the dead alien at our feet, these aliens carried long rifles. Every single one of the weapons was pointed at us.

"Daniel, be careful," X warned in my head. "I know you can heal from almost anything, but we have no idea what they're going to fire at you."

I nodded, letting X know I heard her.

The aliens surrounding us parted ranks for who I presumed was their leader. This alien didn't carry a weapon or have a helmet. It did, however, wear dull gold armor and a purple cloak, unlike the rest of the aliens around us.

He, it—I wasn't sure what to call it at the moment —stared at us with six eyes full of contempt. The eyes themselves had no pupils that I could see, just ebony orbs.

"What's the play here?" I asked Preacher. I slowly lowered my knife and axe, placing them in my belt. My right hand went to the handle of my MK II at my side. I didn't draw it yet in fear that would start another fight, but I was ready.

"Don't know if there's much of a play to be had," Preacher replied. "We try and talk our way out, and if that doesn't work, we fight our way out."

The lead alien clicked something as if he were asking a question. He stared intently at Preacher and me as if we were supposed to understand.

"Don't speak your language," I responded with a shake of my head and a shrug. If my words didn't get through, maybe my actions would tell them what I meant.

The lead alien clicked something again that sounded like he was disappointed or maybe disgusted. It was hard to tell.

The aliens around us lifted their rifles, taking aim.

"What! No—"

Preacher's words were the last thing I remembered. Something hard knocked me to the ground. My body felt numb and tingly as I fell into unconsciousness.

FOR THE SECOND time in recent memory, I woke in a cell. Unlike Sam's prison in the city of Cecile, this one was an actual cave. Or at least what looked like a cave. I sat up stretching aching muscles and working my jaw up and down.

My weapons were gone.

I studied my surroundings, taking in Preacher, who stirred beside me. We were alone, at least as far as I could tell. The cave cell that held us was a side room with poor lighting. The only illumination was from some kind of energy shield that kept us imprisoned.

The light green energy shield gave off a faint buzz.

I concentrated, looking in the darker corners of the room. The night vision I had become accustomed to using was gone. I tried again, but instead of my vision going gold to see in the dark, there was nothing there.

"X, my night vision isn't working," I said, squinting as I tried one more time. "What happened?"

Silence.

Dread filled me as I reached a hand to the back of my neck where X's implant connected us. She was gone.

I sat in the room in shock. X wasn't just an asset to me; she was a friend. I didn't realize how much I relied on her until she wasn't there. Worse, my mind wandered to what could have happened to her.

X, where are you? I wondered. *Hang in there. I'm coming. I'll find you.*

"I'm sorry, *mijo*," Preacher said, slowly standing up. He looked down at me. "I'm sorry for getting you into this mess."

"I'm a big boy," I countered, also rising to my feet. "I didn't do anything I didn't want to do. Plus, you were right. Aliens have come to Mars, as strange as that sounds."

Preacher pursed his lips, looking around the dark cell made from cave rock.

"I'm guessing we're in the mountain or maybe even underground somewhere," Preacher said. He scratched the stubble on his chin. "We'll find a way out. There's always a way out."

I walked over to the light green energy shield that spanned the length of our cell. It reminded me of the same kind of tech that kept Echo in his cell in the Phoenix prison.

"They take that AI of yours? X?" Preacher asked.

"She's gone," I confirmed, reaching out a tentative hand to the energy shield. I had to test it sooner or later if we were going to try and get out of here.

"I wouldn't if I were you." An old woman's voice made me jump in surprise. I wheeled around to the darkest corner in the cave. "You'll get cooked like a bad dinner."

"Who are you?" Preacher demanded to the dark corner of the room. "Come out so we can see you."

"You come out so I can see you," the old woman cackled. "I'm just playing. Forgive an old woman a bad joke. It's been a long time since I've had visitors."

The form that shuffled out of the dark corner was more hair and cloth than a person. An ancient woman with more wrinkles than I could count walked forward. Her left hand supported her along the rough cave wall.

She wore some kind of heavy coat. She was tall or at least had once been tall. She walked with a stoop now. She looked up at us through a curtain of wild dirty hair. Despite the rest of her appearance, her eyes were bright.

"Who are you?" I asked. "How long have you been here?"

"Well, I have a feeling those are two questions in a

very long conversation of questions to come." The old woman did her best at straightening up. "My name is Rosemary Cripps. I've been here for two years now, at least I think it's been two years. You know how time passes in the darkness, or maybe you don't."

"Two years?" Preacher exclaimed in shock.

"Yes, is there an echo in here?" Rosemary asked. "I said I think it has been two years. You can call me Rose, by the way. All my imaginary friends do."

Rose took a moment to do a little curtsy in the rags she was dressed in.

"We underestimated how many years they've been here," Preacher thought out loud. "We had no idea."

"Oh yeah, they've been here much longer than that if I had to guess," Rose said with an exasperated sigh. "Please try and keep up. The Voy have been here three, maybe even four years, growing and preparing their assault."

"Growing?" I asked.

Rose gave me a look that said, "Really? You too?"

"Sorry, didn't mean to echo you," I said. "Just shocked. It's my first time seeing an alien. Before today, I just thought they were fake news in the tabloids."

"Oh, they are as far as the public and the Galactic Government are concerned." Rose shrugged.

"Everyone is so caught up in the latest trend or tech that they're missing what's right under their noses."

"How do you know they are called the Voy?" Preacher asked excitedly. "What else can you tell us about them?"

"I've just heard them use that term a lot," Rose admitted. "I don't know much. I think they're just keeping me here waiting for me to die before they cut me open. Maybe I look like I have one foot in the grave already, so they think I'm going soon. Well, trick's on them. They just keep on taking the others they bring in before me."

"What others?" I asked. "Are there other prisoners here?"

"They bring them in every few weeks." Rose tapped a dirty finger on her chin. "Weeks or months? I can't tell anymore. Anyway, they bring them in then take them out eventually, and I never see them again. I'm just guessing they're experimenting on them, but who knows really."

"Immortal Corp will come for us," Preacher asserted, narrowing his one good eye. "They knew where I was headed. There's a tracker on my Raptor. They'll come."

"If they can find the cloaked dome," I reminded

him. "Even if they do, how many aliens—or the Voy do you think are here? Hundreds, thousands?"

Preacher looked back at Rose, who was grinning at us as if we had just told a joke.

"You said they're growing them here?" Preacher asked. "What do you mean?"

"Just speculation, really." Rose shrugged. "In the two years I've been here, I've seen a lot of weird and disturbing things. One of which is that new Voy come in not as strong or large as the rest. Within weeks or months—like I said, it's hard to keep track— they mature. Who knows, maybe they're reproducing the old-fashioned way, but it seems to me they're growing much faster than humans."

"How did they get you anyway?" I questioned, going to the shield to take a closer look. It was translucent green. A walkway like a hall lit only by the glowing shield ended in darkness in both directions. "Where did they find you?"

"Oh, that's a crazy story," Rose began, blowing a long puff of air from her lips. "I was exploring this part of Mars. Had too much time and way too much money on my hands. I wanted to see it all. I wasn't getting any younger, you know. Hired an expedition team to take me all over the far side of Mars to explore…"

Rose's voice became quieter and quieter as if she were seeing the events in her mind's eye.

"Rose, you okay?" I asked as she stared at nothing.

The woman was catatonic.

"Rose, Rose," I called, snapping my fingers in front of her face.

"I'll take the nitro caf macchiato, hold the spice and add a shot of hard spike," Rose said, startled. She blinked then looked at me as if she were seeing me for the first time. "Sorry, sorry, I'm back now. It happens from time to time. Where was I?"

"You hired an expeditionary force," Preacher filled her in. "You were traveling the far side of Mars."

"Oh yes, yes," Rose said, licking her cracked lips. "We must have gotten too close to their invisible dome. Before we had time to think, half our number were cut down. They came out of nowhere wearing those invisible cloaks. They captured a handful of us. I'm the only one who's left from that group."

The cold hard truth was laid out in front of us.

"I heard them screaming when they were taken." Rose leaned against the wall for support. Her mouth twitched, remembering the events as if they happened that morning. "I couldn't do anything. I tried the first few times, but I was shoved to the side. They all tried to fight, but it always ends the same. They were taken."

"How long do we have?" Preacher asked, looking around the cave for some kind of hint at an escape. "When do they come to take us?"

"Hmmm?" Rose said, blinking back to the moment. "Let's see, carry the three and add the four. They should be here any moment to take one or both of you. But not me, they never take me no matter how much I beg them to."

As if on cue, the sound of heavy footfalls came from the left side of the cave hall. Not just a single pair of feet but four, maybe five. It didn't take long for us to see a group of Voy marching down the hall.

They wore the same armor that we had seen before. Except this time, instead of any bladed weapons or even a sword, they held long poles.

The poles had to be somewhere around six meters with loops on the ends that sparked with dark black energy.

"Here they come," Rose moaned. "I'm sorry. This is where you go. Now they will take you."

FOUR

MY HEART BEAT like a war drum trying to break free from my chest. I looked over at Preacher. He had the same hard stare in his eye. We knew what we were. If the Voy thought they were going to take us without a fight, then they had another thing coming.

"No matter what happens," Preacher started, clenching his right fist and extending it in my direction. "They can kill our bodies."

"But they can't kill our spirits," I finished, rapping his fist with my own. "Let's make 'em pay."

The five Voy came and stood in front of the cell's shield in a neat line. The one in the middle reached for something at his belt. Some kind of metal remote controller hung beside his hip.

One of his three fingers pressed a button. A

doorway in the shield opened, allowing the aliens to walk in one by one. The entrance extended to the ceiling and was wide enough for both Preacher and me to stand shoulder to shoulder.

Waiting to be attacked wasn't really my style. I refused to just stand there while the Voy entered the cave then took up their desired positions.

I lunged forward, sidestepping the first Voy who stabbed his weapon at me. My opponent was larger, better armored, and had four arms. I was at every disadvantage I could think of. Still, he had a weak spot. His helmet didn't cover his throat before his breast-plate provided further protection.

Its lower two hands were carrying the weapon. Its upper two arms reached for me as I closed in.

I slammed into the alien as hard as I could, taking it off balance. We reached for each other, the Voy trying to grab whatever part of me it could while I went for its throat.

I succeeded in landing a right strike under its chin as it seized my left arm and chest.

It sputtered and choked, staggering back.

A sensation of white-hot immobilizing pain scorched my neck. Another of the Voy had looped its weapon around my neck and pulled me back. Whatever kind of technology ran through the long poles with the loops at the end, it hurt, a lot.

My body felt like it moved in slow motion as I reached behind me for the pole. It felt like I was being stabbed by a thousand pins and needles across my body.

The alien behind me jerked me back as I tried to reach for the weapon behind my head. All the while the aliens clicked yells and screeched in rage or maybe words to one another, I couldn't tell.

In my peripheral vision, I could see Preacher fighting. He stood over one bloody alien as the other two sought to secure each of his hands with their energy pole weapons.

I couldn't think of Preacher at the moment. I had to get out of my own situation before I could offer help.

The alien behind me jerked the pole, sending me off my feet and shocking me at the same time. My hands slammed into the sandy ground of the cave. My right palm hit something hard. A rock. It wasn't large, about the size of my fist, but it would do the job.

I picked up the rock and turned. Lifting it, I threw it as hard as I could at the alien securing me. The rock hurtled through the air and hit its mark dead center. The stone made a dinging sound as it bounced off the helmet. It wouldn't do any lasting damage to the alien, but it was enough to stun it for a second.

I seized my opportunity, ripping the pole away from my enemy. I freed my neck from the steel wire of dark force. As soon as the loop was over my head, I felt a sense of relief.

I looked over at Preacher, who was on top of one of his attackers, tearing at the Voy like a rabid animal while a third tried to get him off.

"Behind you!" Rose called out.

Both my own assailants were on their feet and about to mount another attack. I reached down for the pole at my feet and went to work.

It was difficult fighting an opponent with four arms but not impossible. Two arms or four, no one liked having an electric pole slammed into their faces and sternums.

The weapon's length and my skill with the pole more than evened the odds. With a flurry of blows to their heads and the joints on their legs and arms, the Voy went down screeching.

I struck one of them so hard on the temple, its helmet actually flew off. I followed that up with a savage strike to the opposite side of its head, sending it into unconsciousness.

The second Voy I fought back-pedaled, reaching for

the controller on its waist. It hit a button. A high-pitched signal skrieked out in all directions.

I winced. It wasn't enough to stop me from pushing the attack, but the sound was ear-splitting.

To my surprise, Rose jumped on the Voy's back, ripping its helmet from its head with an animalistic war cry I didn't know she had in her.

"Hurry, that's the alarm, more will come!" Rose shouted. A second later, she was thrown from the Voy's back and landed in a heap.

I took the opportunity to batter the Voy's face with both sides of the long pole. Using a center grip on the weapon, I was a blur of motion. Black bloody cuts opened up all over its face and head before a final blow sent it down.

I looked behind me to see Preacher panting. He had dark burn marks around his neck and arms courtesy of the energy loops at the end of the pole weapons. Despite his wounds, he had taken down the three Voy that went after him. Thin tendrils of smoke rose off the areas where the burns scorched his body. He had gotten it worse than I had.

Apparently, the Voy thought we would give in to the pain the poles created. But we weren't like any humans the Voy had come in contact with.

Pounding came from the hall along with harsh clicks of the alien speech I didn't understand.

"Hurry, you have to hurry," Rose exclaimed, recovering from her fall. "They'll come in double the numbers."

"Let's go," I called to Rose as I ran to Preacher's side to get him on his feet.

"I'm not going to be able to keep up." Rose shook her head emphatically. "But you need to go right now."

"I'll hold them off as long as I can," Preacher said, struggling to his legs. He shoved me toward the open exit of the cell. "I'm with Rose. I'm not going to be able to keep up. My body needs time to heal. Go to the Raptor. Contact Immortal Corp. Get them down here."

"What?" I asked incredulously. "I'm not going to leave you."

"No time to argue. There's something going on here that cuts deeper than you and I!" Preacher roared. Shoving me out the cell door, he picked up one of the long poles and joined me in the hall. "Go and get help. No room to argue. I'm not asking here. I'm telling you."

I looked at Rose, then Preacher, as if they were taking crazy pills. Everything inside me was ready for another fight. We both had weapons now. We could take them.

I looked up the hall that was lit by white lights set into the wall farther up. What I saw made my stomach fall in my gut. The Voy filled the tunnel like a horde of ants. There were too many to count. They would be here in seconds.

"Go!" Preacher shouted. He never took his eye off the approaching enemy.

I slowly back-pedaled. Every instinct I had in me besides two told me to stay and fight. The two that made me turn and run were, for one, Preacher was right. We needed help. The Galactic Government and whoever else was willing needed to know about the threat.

Second, I wasn't going to leave without X. I didn't know if that made me sentimental, stupid, loyal, a fool, or something in between. Sure, some would just look at her as an AI, but she was more than that to me. She was a friend and those were in short supply these days.

I pounded down the hall as the sounds of battle filled the space behind me. I wasn't sure where I was going. The cave system branched off to my right and left. White lights set into the walls at least meant I didn't have to run in the dark.

Still, I had no idea where I was going. One direction seemed just as good as the next. I tried to stick to the paths that seemed to move upward. If we were in fact underground, I needed to head to the surface.

I made a hard right, following the incline of the ground. I found myself in a square room full of Voy. These aliens weren't armored. In fact, they looked shocked to see me. They stood, hunched over pulsing sacks on the ground. Vein-like tentacles came up from the ground, creating bulging sacks large enough to fit a small Voy inside.

What's more, the Voy in this room didn't resemble the others, at least not exactly. They looked at me, hunched over their work. Some wore goggles to see through. That seemed strange, since the goggles had six lenses to cover their six eyes.

Holy crip, I thought to myself. *Rose was right. They're growing them.*

The pulsing siren that started in the cell had all but died in the distance now.

We just stood staring at one another.

As if time was suddenly stopped then sped up, one of them screeched and pointed a wrinkled finger in my direction.

That was enough for me to turn and sprint back down the hall. I nearly collided with the Voy flooding the cave passage behind me. Apparently, Preacher's last stand had been short lived. I couldn't blame him.

There had to be a hundred filing down that hall, maybe more.

I kicked out, connecting with the center chest piece of the Voy I ran into. It fell backward, just as surprised to see me as I was to see it.

Behind it, a dozen more Voy reached toward me. Some other Voy in the room I just left must have sounded the alarm. That same piercing siren permeated the air around me.

I dodged the grasp of the Voy behind me as I took off at a sprint again. They followed, only steps behind.

You have to get out of here, I screamed to myself over heavy breathing and the sweat dripping from my forehead. *You have to find X and get out of here or Preacher did this for nothing.*

My superhuman speed kept me in front of them, but how long could I travel blindly in the tunnels before I came to a dead end?

I took a hard right at the next T intersection, sprinting into a room lined with massive cages on either side and stacked one on top of the other.

If I wasn't already in some kind of waking horror, I was now. These cages were filled with people. Voy guards stationed in front of the cages looked at me with shock. A moment later, they descended on my location.

Unlike before, I didn't stop running. I charged through the room. The filthy humans inside the cage saw me and started shouting. I was surprised to hear their shouts weren't for help but rather cheers willing me on.

I realized what I must have symbolized for these people: hope. Hope that one of their own had somehow managed to get free. Hope that I would bring help.

I ducked under the pole of one of the guards who got close enough to take a swing. Another swiped low, taking my left leg out from underneath me. The pole hit my shin so violently, I thought for sure it was broken.

I fell to the ground hard.

The Voy descended on me.

FIVE

I HIT THE GROUND, tucking my right arm under my body, protecting my head. I went into a roll on the opposite side of the fall and jumped back to my feet. There were arms everywhere reaching for me.

The sound in the room was deafening. Screams and yells from the prisoners urged me on. Some called the Voy horrible slews of curses I didn't even know existed. Their shouts reverberated through the room.

I shoved the arms close enough to grab me, giving my legs new speed. There was a doorway at the opposite side of the room. Although I had no idea what was on the other side of the door, I had to hope against hope it was a means to my escape.

I slammed into the door with my left shoulder. It burst open. I was in yet another hall illuminated by the bright white lights set inside the cave walls. The sandy floor beneath my feet made running a new lesson in pain.

My lungs burned just as much as my legs as I sprinted up the ever-ascending path. The cave floor went higher and higher. The harsh clicks and screeches of my pursuers slowly began to fade as my super-human speed and endurance kicked in.

Up, up, and up I ran. Sometimes the passageway turned a corner and rose higher still, back and forth like some kind of stairwell. Just when I thought it would never end, I saw a bright light outside a cave mouth.

The light was the sun.

Sucking in a lungful of breath, I forced my body on toward the light. Had I made it? Dare I believe I escaped the Voy? But what about X? Preacher and Rose? I had to go back for them. I would go back once I got help.

Reaching the end of the cave was an act in frustration. I barely managed to slow my forward momentum before falling off a sheer rock cliff.

The cave mouth ended in the side of the mountain thousands of meters up. There was no stairwell, lift, or any way down. It was a sheer drop. My chest heaved, trying to come up with a plan as my pursuers clicked with glee. They had known all along where this path ended.

I looked down to see if there was any way I would survive the fall. I mean, I would probably survive the fall, but would I be in any condition to get up and run after?

It was then I noticed the futility in my plan. Looking down showed me a scene that squeezed all optimism from my heart. I must have been inside the camouflaged alien dome at this point.

Below me, a thousand—no, two, ten thousand Voy looked up. A military base, at least that was what I guessed it was, sprouted around buildings with high domes. Training grounds, armories, storage facilities— at least that was what they looked like to me-- stretched on and on.

This wasn't an invasion, at least not yet. This was the growth of an army, of an intergalactic fighting force.

Screams from behind me told me I had more pressing matters to deal with.

The Voy chasing me had reached me. Time was up.

"You didn't run all this way just to give up now," I said to myself out loud. "Time to see what you're made of."

I turned to see the Voy running at me from below.

The cave was filled with the alien soldiers. Most of them held those sparking lances with the dark energy loops at the end.

I couldn't see their eyes, but I felt their frustration as they attacked. They were used to being the apex predator. Not anymore. Not with me.

The first Voy was much too eager to poke me with his pole. I used that against him. I sidestepped his attack then grabbed the pole below the black hoop, jerking it past me.

The Voy's own forward momentum sent him over the edge. An ear-piercing shriek left its mouth as it fell to its death. I grabbed the next alien, pivoting my whole body, and tossed it over my hip to follow its comrade to its death.

There were too many of them now. It wasn't like they were lining up to attack me one at a time. The only thing that saved me was that only two aliens could stand shoulder to shoulder in the cave. Plus, it wasn't like they could surround me. My back was to the cliff.

I traded blows, trying in vain not to get caught by their poles. Sharp, sick sensations cracked against my body anytime a black hoop made contact with my skin. It was soon clear they had orders to take me in alive.

Not once did they try and bully me back over the cliff.

I struck out, bloodying my own knuckles on their helmets and hard bodies. Against overwhelming odds, I did what I was made to do. To be honest, a part of me even enjoyed it, as sick and strange as that might sound. That animal I was created to be raged within.

I held them for minutes, which might not seem like a long time, but ask anyone who's been in a long, drawn-out fight. It feels like an eternity. I had already sent two Voy over the edge. Another was on the ground from a series of kicks I sent to his left leg. I heard something snap and he went down screeching.

Another Voy tried to be cute and skirt around me. I sent that son of a gun on a one-way trip down the mountain, in first class.

I couldn't deny it was over. There was no way for me to escape. Sooner or later, they'd hook one of their loops around my hand, foot, or neck and that would be the beginning of the end for me.

Then it happened. Bleeding from a dozen different scrapes and cuts, I front-kicked a Voy who was getting a little too brave. I sent him reeling back into his comrades. The Voy next to him looped his pole around my extended foot.

I lost my balance and the Voy pounced.

"I'm going to live through this," I said regaining my feet in time to get tackled by the Voy in front of me. "You won't."

The alien wrapped its four arms around me, trying to drag me back into the cave. I shoved off the side of the cliff as hard as I could. One second we were struggling for dominance on the edge of the cliff, the next we were falling through the sky.

The strange thing about falling from such a height is that your brain struggles to keep up with exactly how fast you're falling. There's no way to measure your fall. I just knew we were speeding toward the ground. When we hit it, I couldn't be on the bottom.

As we fell, we struggled for dominance. I ripped the helmet off the Voy who held me, smashing the piece of armor against its face. I positioned myself on top of him as we plummeted ever closer to the ground.

There was fear in those six eyes of his, or hers—I really had no idea. Fear, it was the first time I had seen that emotion on any of their faces. That look meant humanity had a chance. If we could instill a little fear in them now, maybe they would think twice about trying to end our race.

After we struck the ground, I don't recall a whole lot. I remember hitting hard, then bits and pieces as I was surrounded then dragged a far distance to some kind of holding cell. I blacked in and out of consciousness during this time.

When I came to, I was sitting in a room full of what looked like medical equipment. Tubes and clean silver tools lined tables along the walls.

I was secured to a steel chair with metal braces that locked my wrists behind my back and to the chair itself. My ankles also had the same braces held tight to the legs of the chair.

I tried to wiggle with no budge in the braces.

It was then I realized that not only had I survived the fall, but my body had already mostly healed itself. I was sore with most of the pain coming from my chest and shoulder, but nothing that would give me pause from getting into another fight.

I looked up from my seat to see a pair of Voy soldiers at the door. They stood stock still. When I started to move, one of them rapped on the door between them.

A moment later, the door opened and a slender Voy came in. Unlike the other aliens I had seen, this one had a feminine touch to it, if that was possible. It wore no armor, carried no weapon.

It was dressed in a long tunic of cream and white. If I had to guess, it was a female.

Another Voy walked in after. This one, like the

former, wore no armor, but a scowl rested on its face. Its robes were dark red and black.

They studied me for a long moment. In turn, I looked back at them, unflinching.

"Are we going to have a staring contest all day or is something about to happen that I should be aware of?" I couldn't help but ask despite them not being able to understand me.

The shorter, angrier-looking one glanced at its counterpart for direction. The taller, slender Voy nodded.

"What are you?" the shorter Voy asked in a deep raspy voice. "You are not human."

My eyes widened. I had no idea these Voy could not only understand me but were capable of speaking English. My shock must have shown clearly on my face because the angry Voy laughed out loud.

"You think we are incapable of learning the dialect from such a primitive species as your own?" he asked, rolling all six of his eyes. That was something to see. "We have been on Mars for years now abducting your own species and learning from them. Didn't take long to understand the dialect really."

"Why are you here?" I asked. "What do you want with us?"

"Our question first," the same Voy said. "What are you?"

"I'm human," I answered.

"Lies!" the Voy exclaimed. "We saw you fall. No human can endure a fall like that. Trust us, we've tested that theory. We thought there was only one subset of humans, but you prove there is another. There exists a warrior race of humans we were not aware of. Explain this to us."

I didn't say a word. If the Voy thought there was in fact a large section of humanity with abilities like my own, maybe it would give us the upper hand.

"Answer me!" The Voy leaned in close, screaming in my face. I could smell rank breath from his mouth.

I turned my head, sucking in a long draught of air. "Your breath is disgusting. Ever heard of flossing?"

"Jokes and humor." The Voy struck me across the face with one of his four hands, then did it again, opening a shallow cut on my lip. "Others of your kind had jokes. They all told us what we wanted to know… eventually. It was only a matter of time. A matter of how much pain they wanted to endure. Tell me, human, do you like pain?"

"It doesn't have to be like this," the taller Voy who had yet to speak finally said. Her voice was softer, a touch higher. "My name is Talia and my counterpart here is Dall. You can spare yourself a lot of discomfort if you just tell us what we want to know."

"No can do," I said with a shrug. "I have a bad memory for these types of things, you see. Too many concussions."

Talia crossed both pairs of arms over her chest. She didn't say anything, but her eyes narrowed.

"That's fine. They all talk, some sooner than others. Everyone talks, given enough pain applied," Dall said with a wicked grin. "Bring in the tool."

SIX

I TOOK by the wicked look in his eyes that the "tool" he was referring to wasn't going to be a tape measure or a level. I could only imagine the kind of torture devices an alien race like the Voy would have. My future looked pretty grim at the moment.

"Wait," Talia said with a raised finger in the air. "I have an idea. Before you go to work on him, let him talk to the AI. She has at least seen the truth. Maybe she can convince him."

Dall didn't looked pleased with the idea. In fact, he looked downright disappointed.

"You can try." Dall finally yielded. "But no more postponing the inevitable when this doesn't work. I know his kind. He responds to only one thing: pain."

Talia reached one of her hands into her cloak and

came back with a circular pad about the size of my palm. The piece of metal had markings on it I didn't recognize. What did catch my eye was the chip in the center of the piece of technology. It was X's chip.

Talia placed the piece of metal on the ground in front of me and pressed one of the markings on the circular piece of tech. A second later, a holographic image of X stood in front of me. She was human size, just like I remembered her in Echo's memory and in my own.

X stood five feet nothing with dark hair and skin tight blue bodysuit. Her face was weary like I had never seen before. She didn't look scared, but the fatigue on her face was unmistakable.

"X," I said. "X, are you okay?"

"Daniel," X said, her eyes full of concern. She turned to Talia on her left. "Why is he secured like this? You said you wouldn't hurt him if I helped you."

"And we haven't," Talia answered. "He tried to escape and we restrained him. That is all. It appears you haven't been as forthcoming as we thought, however. Daniel, here, possesses an ability to fight and heal unlike anyone we've ever seen."

"That doesn't matter," X said, shaking her head. "That wasn't in our agreement. I help and you let him go. That was the deal."

Talia looked at Dall. "We have the other one with the one eye who possesses these same abilities. If Daniel agrees to our terms, I think we can still let him go. Despite the AI having kept the truth about them hidden."

"No, no absolutely not," Dall retorted with a furious shake of his bald head. "The agreement we struck with the AI did not take into consideration what these two are. Had we known they were something other than human, we would have never agreed to her terms."

"What terms?" I interrupted, craning my neck to try and look into X's eyes. "X, what have you done?"

X hung her head. She wouldn't look at me and that was answer enough.

"I had to try and get you out of here, Daniel," X answered. "It's more than just my programming to help you. You're my friend. I'd do anything for you."

I could feel anger boiling inside me, raging to get out and express itself in physical form. I rattled the manacles behind me, trying in vain to free myself. The steel cut deep into my skin.

"There is that animal that lives inside of him," Dall observed, more curious than anything else. "I wonder if that animal can be extracted and put into our own warriors. I wonder."

"What did you tell them, X?" I asked again after recovering from my burst of anger. I calmed my voice. "X, what did you tell them?"

"They said they would let you go," X contended. Her shoulder-length black hair fell down her face like a curtain when she looked up. Those bright blue eyes of hers pierced my own. "I told them everything. We have no chance here, Daniel. I've seen what they are. I've seen the mass of their army. They're a species that has lived thousands of years longer than humans. They've united under one banner. They outnumber us, are better equipped, and carry tech we can only dream about."

My mouth went dry as X listed off the reasons humanity didn't stand a chance.

"They've been here for years studying humans," X continued. "This is their forward base. They have hundreds of thousands of warriors here already. They're growing more and more warriors by the day. Mars has no chance against them, but there's a chance we can come to an agreement with them."

"X," I said, swallowing hard. I already had a feeling I knew what she was going to say. "No."

"It can work," X answered. "They only want to rule over us and use a percentage of the population as a workforce."

"Earth, the moon, Mars are all useless," Dall said, entering the conversation again. "The only resource we want is humanity itself. There are other more profitable planets in the galaxy. We'll transport your species to those where you will do work for us, mining those resources. No one has to die. No one has to even be enslaved if they agree to work for us. Think of it as employment."

"That's funny that you use those words," I drawled. "I wonder what all those prisoners locked in cages would have to say about being enslaved."

"They are a means to a better end," Dall answered. "We required subjects to test to understand your biology and anatomy."

"You wanted to find out the best way to kill us." I stared daggers at him. "You used those people you've abducted over the years as experiments."

"If humans refuse to live on their knees, then yes, we are prepared to kill as many as necessary until those who remain see the error of their ways," Dall revealed as if he weren't speaking madness and instead quoting simple logic. "We will do what needs to be done."

"Trust me, Daniel," X said. I wasn't sure if she could cry, but she looked as though tears were about to slide down her cheeks at any moment. "If there were another way, I would have tried. There are too many of them."

"We just require your cooperation," Talia announced. "Yours to tell us what you are and your species to fall in line."

"Daniel," X implored. "Just give them what they want. Tell them what they want to know."

"Odds," I said, looking X in her eyes. "Tell me the odds on humanity's survival if we fight."

"They are so low, they are nearly nonexistent," X said.

"Tell me, X," I urged.

"The chance that humanity will survive a war with the Voy are point zero, zero, zero seven, five, one. And you should really remember this next number," X winked at me. Neither Talia nor Dall caught the exchange. "One, two, seven point four, five, two are the odds of survival if humanity obeys the Voy, they can climb out of this *HOLE*."

It took me a second to understand what she was talking about. By the wink, I knew she was passing along information, but it wasn't immediately obvious that X was reminding me of the channel for connecting with the Galactic Government contact we had met on the dropship to Earth.

Captain Zoe Valentine was a high-ranking officer

currently stationed at the Hole in New Vegas. It was a long shot, but if I could get a message to her, then maybe we could at least warn the rest of mankind what was coming.

"That's enough," Talia said, narrowing her six eyes. She looked suspicious. There was no way she could tell X was feeding me information, but she knew something was amiss.

"Don't worry about me," X said in a rush of words as Talia moved to turn her off. "I'll be fine if you can get out of here then g—"

"X!?" I shouted as she disappeared.

I gritted my teeth. My vision turned a hint of red. I strained again against the manacles that still didn't budge. It just felt good to give my anger an outlet.

"You heard it yourself, from someone you trust," Talia said. "The odds against you are astronomical if you do not fall in line. All you need to do right now is tell us what you are, how many like you exist, and we can avoid the—unpleasantries."

I reined in my anger, breathing heavily out of my mouth.

"This whole good praetorian, bad praetorian routine you have going on is really cute and all, but if you don't let me go, I'm going to free X and shove that little hologram tech down your throat," I threatened, looking at Talia.

Talia sighed.

"Well, don't say I didn't try to help." Talia turned to leave the room with a look to a grinning Dall. "He's all yours. I'll have them send in your equipment."

A wide smile split Dall's face. As far as I could tell, the Voy had nonexistent lips and little to no teeth.

"Between you and me, I was hoping you'd decide to do this the hard way," Dall admitted as he rolled up the four sleeves that covered his arms. "It was so fascinating to cut open humans as this all started and see what made them tick, but as you can imagine after a few years and hundreds of test subjects, I started to get bored. But with you, Daniel, you are something special."

Dall paused as a pair of warriors carried in a silver case between them.

Dall went through a series of hard clicks, directing the warriors where to place his equipment. Another round of direction from Dall and both the guards at the entrance to the room as well as the pair who brought in the steel case left.

"Where was I?" Dall asked me as he made his way over to his case.

"You were telling me how special I am," I quipped,

preparing myself mentally for what was about to take place. "I think you were going to kiss me or something next."

Dall looked at me with a crazy grin on his lips.

"I like you, Daniel Hunt," Dall said, opening the top portion of the silver case from the middle.

I couldn't see what was inside just yet. I wasn't sure I wanted to.

"I am so looking forward to getting a look inside of you," Dall continued. "That fall you took was a thing of wonder. Everyone thought you were dead. Not just that, the way you and your one-eyed friend fight is another thing of wonder. I'm not sure if even our best grown warriors would be able to keep up with you one on one. Actually, I'm sure they wouldn't be able to."

Dall came back to me with a pair of long tweezers, holding a squirming insect that looked like some kind of pissed-off centipede with hairy pincers.

"This is called a doctoid," Dall explained, lifting the insect right in front of my eyes. It couldn't be longer than my pointer finger. "They are a species that live on my home planet. Complex creatures when you really get to know them."

We both stared at the squirming insect. Dall with eyes of wonder, myself with eyes of trepidation.

"They infiltrate their host, attaching themselves to

the breathing tube. They'll constrict around your throat, giving you the feeling of suffocating then relax, allowing you to breathe, then the process starts over and over again as they feed off your insides. You see they rely on you to live as their food source, so they don't want to see you die, but if you try and remove them, they'll choke you from the inside out."

"Wonderful," I said, clenching my jaw. I knew what Dall wanted from me. He wanted to see the fear in my eyes. He wanted me to beg and plead to let me go. Not me. Not ever. "So is this doctoid going to buy me a drink or two at least before we get to know each other better?"

Dall didn't get the joke, or if he did, he didn't find it very amusing. He placed the creature on my shoulder then stepped back with a grin on his ugly face to watch the show.

SEVEN

I'D BEEN through a lot of pain in my life. Some of it I remembered, most of it I didn't. This kind of pain was different.

The doctoid used its pincers to cut through my shirt and into my shoulder. That in and of itself wasn't so painful. I felt the insect squirm into my body. I did my best not to give Dall the satisfaction of seeing me freak out.

Easy, Daniel, I coached myself in my mind. *You'll get out of this and find a way to kill this thing inside of you. You aren't going to die now. You have to find a way out for X, Preacher, even Rose.*

It was the strangest feeling to sense a creature crawling under my skin then coming to attach itself around my throat. Dall was right in everything he promised. I felt tiny pricks around my throat as the doctoid settled in and set up shop.

My breathing became constricted and shallow. Each breath meant I got half the oxygen I had before. The air came in through my mouth in wheezes.

"There we are, there we are," Dall coaxed soothingly. "The doctoid will help take off the edge. What I'll do now is the real fun part."

Dall went to his case and came back with a small knife in one hand. The end was shaped like a spade. In his other hand, he held tweezers and a small empty glass vial.

"Let's see how you manage to heal, close up, and of course, we'll need samples," Dall said, reaching for my right arm. "Tissue and blood samples will do for now, but I'm sure we'll want bone marrow tests soon."

He went on and on and on. I was wondering if just listening to him talk was part of the torture.

While he made cuts into my arm, I took my mind somewhere else.

I understood the mind was a powerful tool. If I fixated on not being able to breathe, then panic would set in. If I concentrated on how Dall was cutting me open, then the pain I felt would be that much worse.

They can't kill my spirit, I told myself in my head over

and over again. *They can do what they want to my body, but they can't touch my spirit.*

I thought of Amber, of X, of the members of the Pack Protocol. I thought about my memory of how Wesley Cage had come to save me. I focused on anything that would take my mind off not being able to breathe and the pain coming from my right arm.

I could feel my own hot blood dripping down my arm to splatter on the ground below.

Dall kept making his remarks like "so fascinating" or "truly amazing."

When I got my hands on him, I was going to show him exactly what I thought, but now I needed to survive. I grimaced but refused to cry out when he dug the blade into my arm, cutting out the tissue sample.

After what felt like an hour, Dall stepped back. He had filled his tube with enough blood and tissue to keep him happy for a while.

"You are something special," Dall acknowledged, looking from me to the tube in his hand. "Even now your body is working to heal itself from the cuts I made. I can't wait to test these samples then go and see how the older one with the one eye fares under a similar trial."

"I'm getting really tired of hearing you talk," I

wheezed. "Is that some third form of torture you had planned?"

Dall smiled, looking at me with eyes full of wonder. "Amazing. At death's door and you are still as courageous as ever. I can only hope that we can harness whatever healing power you possess and give it to our own warriors. Then we would be truly unstoppable."

That made me feel sick to my stomach more so than the insect in my throat or my right arm cut to ribbons. If Dall was able to somehow figure out what Immortal Corp did to me and do the same to the Voy soldiers, humanity had less than a slim chance.

Dall left me in the dark, shutting off the lights behind him and closing the door. He looked as happy as a kid getting to open up a gift-wrapped present a day before Christmas.

I sat alone in the dark testing my restraints again. Still nothing. The chair was bolted to the ground, my steel bonds secured to the chair.

I studied the room, looking for a way out. If there was one, I didn't see it. But that didn't mean I was giving up.

Giving up was never an option.

I needed to think, but trying to do so was nearly impossible as I struggled to breathe. My chest felt tight, my throat tighter.

I wasn't sure if I was getting lightheaded from the lack of oxygen or something else, but as the minutes turned to hours, I began to hallucinate. I had no idea how long I was in the room.

I saw the door to the room open all on its own then close. My mind was going. Sweat poured down my face. I wasn't sure if the room was getting hotter or this was how my body was reacting to so little oxygen. I was staving off the panic but just barely. The doctoid felt like it was getting tighter around my throat.

I heard footsteps in the dark room. Another trick of my oxygen-deprived mind.

You're losing it, I thought to myself. *You're losing it, hold on. You're not dead yet. X would tell you not to give up. X wouldn't let you give up.*

"You look horrible. Why are you sweating so much?" a woman's voice asked in the darkness. "What did they do to you, Danny?"

I looked up, sure I was hallucinating now. The voice sounded familiar in the same kind of way that déjà vu reminded you of a previous event.

My breathing came in short ragged inhales. I searched the dark room to no avail.

"I'm going to see if I can get you out of these cuffs," the voice said again. "Can you talk?"

"Who—who are you?" I asked, feeling someone

start to work on the cuffs that connected my wrists to the back of the chair.

"Right, you don't remember a thing about us," she said. "I bet you don't remember the fifty credits you owe me either, then? Did I say fifty? I meant five hundred."

I didn't answer. My mind was so far gone, I wasn't sure what to think at the moment. Either I was making all of this up or someone had been sent to help.

A click behind me opened the manacles at my wrists. A dark figure I could barely see moved over to my feet. It was a woman. She was muscular with dark hair tied behind her head.

At first, I thought it could have been the Cyber Hunter, but the build was wrong as well as the voice.

While the woman worked on freeing my ankles, I moved a hand up to touch my throat. The insect flinched and squeezed tighter, making me cough.

"You get the black lung or something while you were here?" the woman asked, freeing my ankles with a click of the cuffs. "Bingo."

"There's—there's an insect around my throat," I managed. "We have to—cut it out."

"Wow," the woman said, taking a step back. "Are you sure you didn't get drugged or something just to think that? I mean, I'm not the squeamish type. Trust me, I've done some pretty messed-up stuff in my day. I'll cut you if you want, but you sure about this?"

"It's going to—to kill me," I said, pointing a finger where the insect was located around my throat. "You'll have to do it fast."

"We've done a lot of crazy stuff in the past, but this one just might take the cake," the woman said, flicking on a small torch in her hand. The beam of light cut through the darkness like nothing.

I blinked a few times, readjusting my eyes to the brightness. I had a better look at her now. She had a checkered crimson and white bandana around the top of her forehead to keep her hair back. She was more muscular than I thought, with a wide face.

She wore a tight-fitting black suit with combat boots and a harness over her chest that carried an assortment of weapons.

This woman had to be one of the two members of Pack protocol I had yet to meet. This was Angel.

She lifted an eyebrow. As I studied her, she was taking a look at my neck.

"Well, you're not wrong," she said. "I can see a bulge right around your Adam's apple that doesn't belong there. I can cut it out, but it's going to bleed a lot and not feel great."

"Do it," I croaked.

"Hold tight," Angel said, producing a short-bladed knife from her vest. She handed me the torch. "Hold it still."

I pointed the light at my neck, mentally preparing myself to willingly have my throat slit .

With a single graceful move, Angel opened up my throat. I could feel the doctoid wiggle and shiver as it tried to wrap its body tighter around my throat.

Angel reached in and ripped the insect out.

With my left hand still holding the torch, I slammed my right hand over my bleeding throat. Hopefully, I could stem the loss of blood while my body healed.

I shone the light at Angel, who held the insect in one gloved hand. The blood-soaked doctoid wiggled and then tried to position its pincers to have a go at Angel.

"Sorry, little guy. It's just not your day," Angel said, tightening her fist and squashing the insect in her palm.

As if the scene couldn't get any more disgusting, the insect's outer shell gave to the force of Angel's grip. With a wet crunch, the doctoid turned to mush in her hand.

I sat in the chair, one hand slowing the flow of my blood, the other shining the light at Angel.

A dozen questions crashed through my mind at once. It wasn't like I could ask any of them with my throat still healing.

Angel turned to me with a grin.

"So good to see you." She extended a hand toward me covered in insect juice. "Angel aka Archangel, aka number six."

EIGHT

I ACCEPTED the offered hand with my own that still held the torch light. I didn't trust myself to let go of my bleeding throat just yet. I knew I healed fast, but I needed a few more seconds at least.

"Looks like you've got your hands full not bleeding out, so I'll run the conversation for now," Angel said. "Hold that throat."

Angel pressed a finger to her right ear. "I have Danny. We're going to get him on his feet and then head for Preacher. Maintain your position."

Someone must have said something over the comm line to her approval because Angel removed her finger and turned to me.

"I can give you a few minutes, but then we have to

move," Angel told me. "Do you know where they're holding Preacher?"

"In the mountain," I croaked. "A tunnel system underneath."

Angel pursed her lips. I could practically see the wheels turning behind her dark eyes.

She broke into an unexpected wild grin a minute later.

"We've been through a lot: mutated grunts, that crazy scientist on the dark side of the moon, and the rogue AI, but aliens? This one takes it all," Angel said with a short chuckle. "Have to laugh about it or it's enough to shove you into an early retirement in the loony bin. Am I right?"

I cleared my throat, finally taking my hand away from the wound. To my relief, no new wave of blood gushed out. It seemed I had healed enough to at least close the cut.

"How are you here?" I asked, deciding on that to be the first of many questions I had. "How did you know?"

"Immortal Corp tracks all their vehicles," Angel said, accepting the torch I handed back to her. "When Preacher missed his check-in, it was clear there was something wrong. He never misses a check-in. Spartan was able to track you and then we found the dome."

"How did you find it?" I asked, remembering the way it was concealed to the naked eye.

"Tracks, again," Angel responded. "It was clear where they took you. We cycled through a number of viewing modes before we could find you, but it worked. After that, I camouflaged in here and now here we are."

"Camouflaged," I said, repeating the word. "You mean you turned invisible?"

"Yeah, you don't remember anything?" Angel asked with a raised eyebrow. "They really scrambled your brain, huh? The testing we went through to make us heal faster changed us all. You heal the fastest and can take the most damage. I can camouflage into pretty much any setting."

Sam didn't tell me this part, nor did I see her use any kind of different ability while we fought in Cecile. Neither did Preacher use an alternate means of fighting when I fought alongside him.

I wanted to know more about these abilities we had, but now didn't seem like the right time to sit down and have a heart to heart.

Angel had already moved to the door. She put her ear to it now.

"There are two guards out there," she said. "I made a noise down the hall that drew them away just long enough for me to sneak past and get to you. We'll have to take them out now."

"I'm ready for some payback," I promised. "But one more thing. They have cages and cages of humans here. We can't go without them and I'm not going without my AI, X."

Angel gave me a hard stare. "You're overcooking my grits here. We'll do what we can. But we stay on mission. My mission was to get you and Preacher out of here. Second to that, we secure proof of the alien invasion. That's it."

"You do what you got to do," I said. I had no intention of leaving those people here to die. Angel read that in my tone.

"Man, wipe your memory and you turn into a saint." Angel handed me the hilt of the blade she had used to cut the doctoid out. "Here, you still good with a blade?"

"I'll make it work," I said, accepting the weapon.

"Good, I'll take our visitor from another planet on the right, you take the one on the left," Angel instructed. She pulled out a handgun from behind her back. The weapon had a short but thick suppressor on the end. "We'll need to move fast. Daybreak isn't far off. We'll need to be out of here before then."

"I'm with you," I said, holding the knife so the blade pointed down.

Angel placed her hand on the door, about to push it open, then she paused.

"Daniel," she said, looking back to me in the darkness. "I'm sorry."

I knew exactly what she meant. This was the first time she had seen me since Amber's death.

"So am I," I said.

Angel nodded then opened the door.

The guards on the opposite side had zero chance. Not only were they not expecting to be attacked, but they were certainly not expecting to be attacked from behind.

I went straight for the guard's throat, slamming my blade up into the underside of his jaw and driving it in as deep as I could. The Voy's four arms flailed and grabbed at me, but it was already over.

The alien slumped to the ground in a puddle of black blood.

I looked behind me to see Angel had taken out her alien with a pair of rounds to the chest. Her weapon was completely silent. It had to be something new, some kind of cutting-edge tech that Immortal Corp set her up with. All the silencers I had ever seen only acted as a suppressant for the sound of the weapon's fire, not a total deterrent.

"Here," Angel said, taking off a long cloak her downed soldier wore. "It's not going to do anything but give us a chance. Still, in the dark and at a distance, it might fool a few of them."

I wasn't going to argue with her. At this point, we needed whatever edge we could get. I tossed the cloak over my shoulders. It was heavy and smelled like rotten flesh, but beggars can't be choosers.

The hood fell over my forehead and we moved on. Angel was there one second then completely invisible the next. She was being modest when she said she could camouflage into nearly anything.

"You're not going to be able to see me, so I'll call out where we're going," Angel said in a rush of words. "Straight down the hall to the door and turn right. It'll take us outside and toward the mountain."

I pulled the rotten-smelling cloak round me tighter. It was a bit too long for me and dragged on the ground. Angel's directions were spot on. We moved down the hall together to the far end where a door sat in the wall.

The alien structure I walked through was clean with greyish white walls and floors. Brightly lit, we passed doors and halls to the right and left of us. All was quiet for the time being.

I was exhausted. Between the loss of blood and lack of sleep, not to mention the torture, my body had been put through the ringer. Right now wasn't the time to stop. We had to free the prisoners which included X and Preacher and somehow get out of here unnoticed.

When we did reach the door, Angel didn't hesitate.

From my vantage point, it was strange to see the door open as if on its own. The steel door had to be eight feet tall and extremely heavy. Still, Angel was able to maneuver it without a problem.

I stepped out behind her, holding the cloak tight around me with one hand and my knife in the other. I walked as tall as I could, straightening my back and even getting on my tiptoes to mimic the height of the Voy.

The cool air hit my face like a gift from above. I could easily see out of the cloaked dome the Voy used to hide their base. What seemed like millions of stars twinkled in a clear sky.

Around me, a small city sprouted in every direction. There were multi-storied buildings, Voy soldiers walking their designated routes, and sounds of heavy machinery at work as the manufacturing buildings toiled day and night, creating the Voy army.

"Hurry," Angel whispered. "Stick to the shadows as much as possible and walk straight to the mountain."

I fought myself not to run and hugged the right side of the building as much as possible. The Voy we did see wore the same long cloaks as I did, but they draped their bodies like they actually fit instead of enveloping them in the fabric folds.

The mountain loomed closer in the night. My heart hammered in my chest. At any moment, we could be found out. I had no doubt Angel and I could give them a run for their money, but in the face of an entire army, our only chance came from stealth and secrecy.

Another Voy patrol down a street to our left then another to our right set me on edge. On both occasions, they were either too far away to notice me or perhaps I did resemble a short Voy just enough that they didn't think anything of it.

For now, there was no reason for them to be on high alert. As far as they knew, both Preacher and I had been recaptured. They had no idea Angel had infiltrated their compound.

That could all change in a matter of seconds. At any moment, someone could stumble across the pair of dead Voy at the entrance of my holding cell. The alarm would sound and we would be forced to fight our way out of the alien complex.

Luck or fate, depending on what you believed in, saw us to the side of the mountain where an open tunnel led inside. Deeper into the interior of the mountain cave, I could see lights set inside the cave walls leading farther and farther back.

That was when the odds finally caught up to us.

A Voy heading out of the mountain cave walked directly toward me. There was nowhere for me to hide or shadows for me to try and conceal my form. The bright stars overhead shone down on me like a spotlight.

With every step the Voy approached, I could see its suspicion rise. I saw its head tilt to the side beneath its helmet. Both its upper two arms clutched the weapon in its hands tighter.

It clicked something I didn't understand in my direction.

I held the knife close to my chest and lowered my head to wrap my face in shadow. I kept moving forward, even when it lifted its weapon in my direction and clicked something else that sounded aggressive.

A second later, it slumped to the ground with a crater the size of my fist in the left side of its head.

Angel had let him have it with her blaster at point-blank range. Even its helmet was useless as a defense that close.

"We have to get the body out of the open, fast," Angel said. Reaching down, she hefted the Voy over her shoulder with a grunt. The woman's physical prowess was beyond impressive. The Voy had to weigh close to two hundred and fifty pounds. "Grab its weapon."

I obeyed as we hurried into the cave entrance that allowed access to the inside of the mountain.

"We need to stash the body and find Preacher ASAP," Angel grunted as she carried the body forward.

"X and the other prisoners too," I added.

Angel didn't say anything.

I knew we were going to butt heads when it came down to it. We were both biding our time until Preacher was found and rescued to have it out.

"Any idea where Preacher is being kept?" Angel asked.

At the moment, she looked more strange than anything I had seen in the recent past and that was saying a lot—I just had an insect inside of my throat. Angel was still invisible with the hefted Voy over her shoulder. It looked like a drunk Voy was floating in the air controlled by some ethereal presence.

"No, I only know that he's either on a lower level

or maybe below the mountain if there are caves that exist down there. When I made my escape, I headed up for what seemed like forever," I answered.

"Well, that doesn't really narrow things down," Angel chided, stopping by a spot in the cave hall where a door on our right led to another chamber. "I've got to stash this body somewhere. This room seems as good a place as any. Care to see what's behind door number one?"

NINE

WE BREACHED THE DOOR.

Angel put the body down and went in first. I still had no real idea on how her ability worked. It seemed that the fabric she wore as well as her weapons were invisible, since I couldn't see her clothes or the weapons she held. Perhaps they were coated in something that reacted to her body's transformation.

Whatever the answer was, it would have to wait.

This didn't seem like the right time to have a heart to heart about her genetics. She went in first, startling four Voy guards who stood in the middle of a room of holographic screens.

The bright display popped up from the ground. All around the room, there were images of the various spaces inside the mountain. I saw the chamber where the cages of slaves were held, the room where the Voy were grown, and finally, the cell where Preacher and Rose lay on the floor.

I took this in at a glance as all four Voy shouted and reached for their weapons.

Seeing Angel work was so strange. First one Voy fell with its skull crushed inward by one of the rounds of her silenced weapon and then the next.

These Voy assigned to desk duty apparently hadn't seen a need to wear their helmets. That was a mistake they wouldn't live to regret.

By the time the last two Voy reached their weapons and turned to fight, Angel was strangling her third target from behind while I slammed my blade in the throat of the fourth and tore sideways. Black blood mixed with tissue painted the floor and the wall beside us.

I bullied my target back, slamming a hand over its mouth as the Voy tried to gurgle a warning.

The alien slumped to the ground, quivering.

Angel ditched her camouflage then ran to the door to carry the initial body in and closed it behind her.

"What are the odds that we would have found the exact room where they monitored the rest of the mountain?" I asked Angel with a raised eyebrow. "How did you know?"

Angel grinned in my direction, tapping her right ear.

"Our eye in the sky has been scanning the mountain," Angel divulged, going over to a control panel that looked like a circular podium with a bunch of buttons to press. "Spartan pointed out this room. He said there were strange power surges coming from it. I guessed it was some kind of tech or control room. I guessed right."

I wiped my blade clean on the tunic of the Voy slumped at my feet. Next, I joined Angel at the control station. To do what, I really didn't know. The control panel had alien symbols I didn't understand along with a myriad of glowing lights that ranged from dark blues to bright greens and crimson reds.

"That's where we need to go," I told Angel, pointing to the prison cell where Preacher and Rose lay. I hoped they were just sleeping and weren't seriously hurt. It was too hard to tell at the moment with the lighting in the cell and the positions they lay in.

"I'm not really well-versed in alien tech these days," Angel said, swiping at a large half ball that rose up from the center console. When she motioned with her hand over the half orb, one of the images in the holographic screens to our right changed.

Instead of the view of the room where the Voy were

grown, it showed an image of the exterior of the mountain. Angel swiped again and again, going through various images.

She pressed a button that went back and then another that went forward. Precious seconds ticked by. One thing was becoming clear; we had no idea what we were doing, and at any time, Angel could press a button on the console that would set off a warning. We were the blind leading the blind at the moment.

"Daniel, is that you?" X's voice came out of the podium where we stood trying to figure out how to reach Preacher.

"X?" I asked with a sense of relief. "X, where are you?"

"I managed to connect to their central console," X answered. "They don't know yet, but they will soon. Daniel, you have to get out of here now."

"Not without Preacher," Angel said.

"Not without you," I said right over her.

"Preacher's two floors down," X answered. "Grab one of the discs on the dead guards in the room. I can speak to you over that piece of alien tech. It looks like the one Talia used in the interrogation room. Daniel, I'm so sorry I couldn't help you. I can't imagine what they did to you."

X's voice sounded pained, like she was feeling

some kind of physical agony just thinking what they did to me.

"I'm fine," I told her. "I'm not going to look at centipedes the same way again, but I'll be fine."

"We have to go now," Angel said. "Get your AI and let's move. Same plan as before. I'll go camo and you wear a cloak."

I nodded, running over to one of the dead Voy and sifting through the heavy belt he wore. I found one of the metal discs and lifted it up for inspection.

"X, are you in here?" I asked.

The disc glowed a dull blue.

"I am," X answered. Her voice sounded heavy, weary even. "I'm still getting a handle on their technology, but it seems they are able to control a large portion of their facility with wireless power. I figured out how to travel from physical object to physical object, but there's still so much I don't understand. Daniel, I have so much to tell you. So much we should be prepared for. We can't beat—"

"We'll figure it out," I told X as I gently placed the pulsing disc in my pocket. "Let's get Preacher and the prisoners out of here and we'll figure out the rest later."

Even though I couldn't see her, I trusted Angel had done her invisibility act and was running right along with me. Navigating the maze of halls in the mountain now was simple.

X called out our route.

"At the end of this hall, you'll see a ramp going down. Take that two floors and then enter the hall. Preacher and Rose are being held in a cell to the left of the hall," X instructed. "There are no Voy between us and them at the moment."

"How long do the Voy sleep?" Angel questioned from somewhere in front of me. "How long until the sun rises?"

"Daybreak on Mars is still hours off, but there is a change in the guard in less than ten minutes' time," X answered. "We'll probably be found out when that happens."

I could hear Angel pick up the speed at which she ran in front of me. I did the same. With no need for silence, we pounded down the hall.

"There will be guards stationed at the opposite end of the hall, but they shouldn't be able to hear you yet," X informed us.

"The prisoners?" I gasped as I ran. "Where are they?"

"Three stories up from our current location," X answered. "The cliff you fell off of when you escaped the first time is another four stories up from there. We

FURY   91

can free the prisoners and lead them to that cave side cliff. If we have transportation off Mars, we can call in the ship to meet us there."

"I'll need directions to give our pilot," Angel responded from somewhere in front of me. "It'll be tight. I can't imagine they'll just let us hop on our dropship and make a run for it."

I was going to ask X if she thought the prisoners in the cages would all be able to fit into the dropship when we reached Preacher and Rose.

They were behind the force field shield. The former opened his one good eye when we approached. The latter lay fast asleep. At least I hoped she was still asleep. I didn't know what it was about the older woman. Something about her put me at ease, told me she was more like me than I would give her credit for at first glance.

"I can open it," X volunteered as Angel appeared in front of a control panel on the right side of the cave wall. "Give me just a minute."

"Spartan?" Preacher asked, standing up.

"Good to see you too," Angel said with a silly grin. "He's got a dropship ready for us."

"It's good to see both of you," Preacher said.

Rose roused herself from sleep and rubbed her

tired eyes. She gave me a goofy grin. "We finally getting out of here or what?"

"There we go," X announced, lowering the shield that kept prisoners in place. "I've located an armor room above us as well. Your weapons are logged in there."

"Let's go," Preacher said, accepting a knife from Angel.

I got a better look at him as he exited the cave. He had a slight hitch in his step. A section of his face looked like it had been burned.

"It's all good," Preacher assured, catching my eye. "I'll heal, just not as quickly as you. Let's make these aliens pay."

"Six minutes until the guards change," X interrupted us. "If you want to get to the armory and then free the prisoners before the alarms sound, it's going to be tight."

"About liberating these prisoners," Angel began, looking at Preacher for some support. "We can come back for them. My mission was to free you and Daniel, then if I was able to secure some proof of the alien threat. Nothing about freeing prisoners."

I looked at Preacher. I got this wasn't some school-room debate. We were all going to do what we thought was best despite what anyone else said.

I wasn't going to leave these people here to get tested on. I knew exactly what Dall was capable of and it left a bad taste in my mouth.

"Will the dropship fit them all inside?" Preacher asked.

"I don't know," I said, trying to remember how many people were trapped in the cells. "Maybe."

"We'll take as many as we can," Preacher decided, heading off down the hall.

Angel looked like she was going to open her mouth to argue. She thought better of it and moved down the passage with us instead.

Our run took us through a wide curve in the hall where Preacher and Angel fell on a pair of Voy so fast, they had no chance. Angel made use of her silenced pistol while Preacher practically sawed the head off the alien he came in contact with.

Rose did her best to keep up, but as we ascended the ramps to the higher halls where our weapons were stashed, it was clear she wasn't going to be able to match our pace.

"Go," Rose wheezed. "I'm an old woman. I'm not meant to sprint like you three. Go, I'll do what I can to hold them off. I'll be fine."

Angel shrugged and turned to go. Preacher at least

looked regretful, but he also seemed to accept this for an answer.

"No, come on," I told Rose, not waiting for permission before I grabbed her and put her on my back. "We're not going to lose someone else. We've lost enough. We've all lost enough."

"What happened to him?" I heard Angel ask Preacher, not that she was trying to mask her question at all.

Preacher didn't answer. Instead, the three of us were off again.

We just made it to the closed door where our weapons were being held when the alarms went off.

TEN

IT WAS LESS of an alarm than a high-pitched, brain-numbing sound that practically bore into my skull. This one was different from the one before. This sound was louder and seemed to come from the walls of the mountain themselves.

"Door's open," X called from my pocket. She was just loud enough to be heard over the siren. "They've found the bodies. They'll realize I was able to gain access in minutes. Hurry."

We ran into the room where not just our own but an assortment of weapons were held. Racks upon racks of alien weaponry stood in front of us as if we were about to go shopping on some other planet.

Our gear was on a table to the left. I let Rose slide down off my back.

"Well, it's been quite a few years since I accepted a ride from a stranger, but thank you, Daniel," Rose said. Her thin lips pressed hard against one another as if she wanted to say more but didn't have the words.

"We're getting out of here together," I told her.

"No need for silence anymore," Preacher said, placing his katana over his shoulder. "Grab some of their weapons. We take as many prisoners as we can and we're out of here."

Preacher looked at me as if he were asking for me to agree.

I nodded.

My MK II was still in its holster. I strapped the hand cannon to my right leg and reached for my axe and knife next.

Angel put her silenced pistol away and went for the largest weapon in the room. It looked like a cannon with six smaller rotating barrels.

Preacher chose a rifle similar to the one used by the Voy who ambushed us.

"X, any idea what passes for an explosive around here?" I asked, sensing the urgency to go. "We need something that goes boom."

"To your left," X directed. "The weapon with the large drum on the bottom and the short barrel."

"Let's go," Angel barked, heading for the door. "Time's up."

I ran over toward the weapons and grabbed one off the rack. It was lighter than it looked. The grip was large for my hands, and instead of a trigger, there was a button, but I got the general idea.

Rose joined me a minute later, hefting a duplicate weapon. She teetered for a moment until she adjusted to the weight.

"Oh my." Rose smiled, feeling the promised power of the weapon in her hands. "I think I'm going to like shooting this."

"Not to interrupt the love fest with your weapons, but aliens incoming," Angel said by the door. She propped open the door for us with her foot. In her left hand, she carried her multi-barrel weapon pointing down. In her right, she held an explosive.

Rose and I made it out the door while Angel released the depressor on her round explosive and tossed it back into the room. She allowed the door to close behind us and we were off.

A thunderous explosion shattered the air a few seconds later, then a dozen more smaller pops and booms sounded as the weapons in the room were destroyed.

I hunched down so Rose could climb on my back

again and we were off. The shadow of the woman weighed almost nothing. I had carried backpacks that felt heavier.

"Down the hall four floors up," X yelled over the siren and the explosions behind us. "They know where we are. I'm locked out. I can't help anymore."

"It's all right. You did enough," I shouted. "You gave us a chance."

"The prison guards will be waiting for us," Preacher shouted behind his back as he and Angel took the lead. "Neutralize them as fast as possible. We free the prisoners and then make a run to the dropship."

"Four floors up," X reminded us.

"Four floors up," Preacher agreed.

Preacher and Angel burst into the level holding the prisoners like chaos incarnate. Prior to this altercation, I had fought alongside Sam and separately Preacher. I had seen what two members of the Pack were capable of. With three of us assaulting the Voy together, they had no chance.

I set Rose down as soon as we entered the room. Angel advanced on the left side while Preacher made for the right. I cleaned up anything in the middle.

The fight was ferocious and short lived. We waded into the enemy fire with impunity. Even Rose, who to my knowledge didn't have the ability of accelerated healing, roared along with us as we cleared the room.

Out of my peripheral vision, I saw her heft the explosive weapon. She pressed the button sending a round into the center mass of a Voy that caved his chest in. The recoil of her weapon sent Rose off her feet and tumbling backward.

I would have thought this was funny if I wasn't so lost in my own blood rage. My right thumb tapped the button to fire the weapon as fast as I could track targets. A round from a Voy slammed into the left side of my chest. I ignored the pain and moved on.

In seconds, the room was cleared. Preacher's weapon smoked.

Angel was securing the door behind us with a booby-trap of her own explosive she produced from the vest she wore.

A mixture of cheers and yells for help came from the humans inside the pens. They were filthy, emaciated, and maybe even diseased. Some of them looked at us in shock, others showed their gratefulness with tears in their eyes.

They were of all races and ethnicities, age and sex. The Voy had done their research, making sure to be thorough and kidnap a wide sampling of humans. There were two rows of cages stacked on top of each other. My heart sank when I did the math. There were going to be too many prisoners to fit inside a single dropship.

Maybe, maybe there was a chance we could pile on top of one another, but I couldn't think about that now. I had to get these people free and we had to go.

As if to emphasize these words Angel's booby-trap at the door went off. My ears rang from the sound of another explosion ripping through the air. The prisoners in their cells screamed.

I traded my heavier alien weapon for my MK II and started blasting the locks on the cells holding the prisoners. I could see Preacher slashing through the bars with his glowing red katana.

A stream of prisoners trampled each other to get out of the cell. A few of the braver ones picked up weapons from the fallen Voy. They looked so weak, it was a miracle they could lift the weapons at all.

The room was full of smoke and dirt.

I lifted myself up to the second round of cells and sent three rounds from my MK II into the locking mechanisms on the metal doors. The cells opened as the prisoners shouted their thanks.

"Get them out of here!" Preacher roared at me. "You know the way. Angel and I will follow."

I didn't argue with him. He was right. Now I just had to remember the path I had run before.

I looked for Rose in the crowded room. In the mass of people, I couldn't see her. I choked on the smoke and dirt coming from the fight as much as from the stench of the prisoners.

Some of them had already taken off through the cell room toward the hall ahead. If there were more Voy on the upper floors, they were dooming themselves to be recaptured or more than likely killed.

I moved on the outskirts of the people in the room, shouting as I ran.

"I know you're scared, but you have to focus!" I yelled. "Follow me. Help those who can't move quickly, but you have to follow me. We have a ship four stories above us waiting. Come on!"

I turned my attention to the path that lay ahead down the hall and up the ramps that led to the upper floors. Behind me, a crush of prisoners followed screaming, crying, numb with emotion.

I could hear Preacher and Angel behind me, urging people forward. I understood why Preacher had given me the job of taking the lead. He was worried I'd stay in the rear helping the slowest get to the ship.

I had to remind myself then what kind of people we were. The person I had been shaped into by

Immortal Corp. I was a weapon. I was a mercenary who looked out for myself and my own. I had been trained to complete missions, nothing more.

Maybe whatever had caused me to lose my memory in the first place had been a hard reset as to the type of person I had been before all the Immortal Corp training.

These thoughts crashed through my mind as I headed up the ramps that crossed back on one another like a stairwell. The lights set inside the cave walls were more than enough to see by.

Ahead, I heard screams and the sounds of alien weapons behind me fired. It seemed like I was right. There had been more Voy in the mountain on the upper levels. How many more was yet to be seen.

"Almost there," X called from my pocket. "One more ramp then straight ahead. I can't see the schematics anymore, but I remember them from before."

Lungs sucking in air, I pumped my legs faster. When I reached the level where the cliff let off, I was greeted by a dozen or more Voy.

You have to beat them, Daniel, I thought to myself as I charged the enemy. *If you don't, then who will?*

The group of Voy stood over the dead bodies of the few prisoners who had managed to make it this far before me. With my right hand on my MK II and my left hand wrapped around the handle of my axe, I charged forward.

A pair of headshots brought their numbers down before I took a round to my midsection. I gasped with pain, pausing for the slightest second before sending a round from my MK II into the face of the Voy who shot me.

Another round from their laser weapons hit me in the left thigh, tearing skin and muscle. I went with the momentum, allowing it to turn my whole body. I twisted, hurling the axe through the air. It slammed blade first into the chest of another Voy.

The axe was hampered by the alien's armor but bit deep enough to send the alien falling backward. The Voy soldier screeched in pain.

More rounds pumped from my MK II and I reached for my blade. I was close enough now to fight them hand to hand. But it was different. Their four arms gave them an advantage I couldn't compensate for in my weakened state. The simple fact was that my body had been through too much, lost too much blood for me to put together a coherent attack strategy to compensate for their extra limbs.

An alien hand grabbed my MK II and another sent its fist into my jaw. I rammed my blade into the unprotected skull of another Voy. Those who remained fell on top of me, crushing me with their sheer numbers.

This was it.

X screamed something at me. I couldn't understand her under the crush of alien bodies pinning me to the ground.

ELEVEN

JUST WHEN I thought it was all over, an explosion blasted not just the Voy on me but me along with them. Fiery hot pain came from the explosion. My own blood dripped into my eyes as I was thrown to the side of the cave. My head bounced off the rock wall.

There was nothing but ringing in my ears at the moment. Despite my battered body, if I could have smiled in that moment, I would have. I witnessed Rose enter the cave hall with her explosive weapon in hand. She was yelling something to the prisoners behind her.

Barely strong enough to lift the weapon on their own, the recently freed prisoners, who'd snatched the downed Voy's weapons, fired on their previous captors with impunity.

I could see the light of hate and dread in the prisoners' eyes. A mixture of trepidation and excitement of being free filled them as they fired on the Voy. Just like the altercation below, this battle was brief but fierce.

The Voy put up a fight, but there were too few left standing after I got through with them. Rose and the prisoners made quick work of the rest. I struggled to my feet, getting strange looks of wonder from the freed humans.

I could only imagine what I looked like. Charred from the explosive rounds Rose fired and bloodied by my own fight with the Voy. I probably looked like a walking corpse to them.

"Sorry, sorry, I got excited with this weapon," Rose said, lugging the thing over to me. "It gives one heck of a kick when I fire it."

"I'll live," I said, looking down at my tattered clothing. The wounds where the Voy rounds hit me were already closed.

"You—got a—you're kind of on fire, still," Rose murmured. "Here."

Rose patted my back a few times and stamped out the tiny flames still eating at what was left of my Voy cloak.

"Thanks," I said, reaching down to my pocket. "X, you still with us?"

"Still here, and just a reminder that we need to go," X answered. "I'm not plugged in to their network anymore, so I can't see their movement, but I imagine every Voy in the compound is heading toward the mountain at the moment."

"Right." I looked at Rose. "Keep leading them down this hall. You'll run into a sheer drop-off. Wait there. A dropship will be coming for us."

"Got it," Rose said. She yelled to those around her, "Come on, we're not out of this yet. If you want to live, follow me!"

Rose hurried down the hall with the mass of survivors behind her. I was on my way back down to see how Angel and Preacher were faring when I noticed a kid kicking the corpse of a Voy.

The kid couldn't have even been a teenager yet. He was filthy from his head to his bare feet. A torn shirt fell off his emaciated frame and pants had been double knotted to stay on his slim waist.

Tears made streaks down his dirt-encrusted cheeks. He stomped on the skull of a dead Voy over and over again, lost in some memory of what had been done to him.

"Hey, kid," I said, checking the ammo in my MK II. "You got to go."

The boy grunted something unintelligible as he slammed his bare foot into the skull of the Voy yet again.

"Hey," I said, taking a knee next to him. I rested a hand on his shoulder. I felt nothing but bone under his shirt. "Hey, kid. He's dead. You have to get going if we're going to get out of here."

"They killed my mother," the boy choked through gritted teeth. "They burned her. They froze my father, experimenting on them. They were going to kill me next."

The boy managed this through sobs. All the while, he smashed his heel into the face of the dead Voy.

"But you're still alive. You'll be able to make the Voy pay for what they did to you and your parents, but only if you get going right now," I told him. "You go and make their sacrifice matter. Hurry, now, go!"

I shouted the last word, ripping the boy free from his past nightmares. He looked up at me, swallowed hard, and nodded. He was off with the rest of the survivors a second later.

"Hey, we got to go!" Angel roared as she and a bloody Preacher made it up the ramp into the hall. "We've got no time! Spartan's at the cave exit."

Clicks and screeches followed Preacher and Angel's appearance. The Voy were close behind.

"I've got enough for one more welcome package," Angel said, unclasping a pair of circular explosives from her vest. "Let's go."

Angel clicked a tiny red button on the top of both of her explosives then tossed them into the hall behind her. All three of us headed down the passage toward the exit.

A resounding boom followed us down the hall as we picked our way over the carnage of the dead Voy..

"Wait, we need proof," Preacher called, stopping to lift one of the Voy corpses. "No one will believe us without proof."

I hefted the Voy over my shoulder, helping Preacher. It was heavier than it looked. How Angel had managed to carry one so easily was still a mystery to me.

"Roger that! Hold on!" Angel yelled into her earpiece.

Preacher and I looked at her for a consensus.

"Spartan's loading the prisoners." Angel rushed us forward. "Small arms fire won't penetrate the hull of the dropship, but it won't be long until the Voy bring out the big guns."

We redoubled our effort, making our way down the

hall to the dropship. We turned a corner and I saw the press of people making their way from the hall to the craft.

Rose was there, urging them on board, as was a large man with a wide chest. He wore his hair in a Mohawk with a thick black beard.

Memories of the man with the call sign "Spartan" crashed into my mind. I had to blink them away to stay on task. As much as I would have liked to, there was too much going on now to sit in my memories.

Spartan and Rose screamed for those loading into the dropship to keep piling in and press to the back. The Voy following us in the caved-in ramp way were clicking and screeching as they tried to dig their way toward us.

We made it to the rear of the mass of humans boarding the dropship. Spartan had to be some kind of ace pilot. He had the dropship hovering in place with its rear door resting on the lip of the cave cliff.

He looked at me and grinned despite the hour. He shouted something at me, but the noise of the dropship's thrusters was too loud to hear him.

A second later, something large collided with the side of the cliff right next to the dropship. The whole mountain rumbled and rolled. I lost my footing and fell with the corpse of the Voy still over my shoulder.

"We've got to go now!" Angel screamed over the press of noises around us. "The Voy below are shooting at us."

"Not before everyone's loaded inside!" I yelled back.

We both looked at Preacher for his decision.

Instead of giving either of us an answer, Preacher hugged the side of the cave, forcing himself to the front of the line. Angel and I followed. When the recently freed prisoners saw who was shoving their way to the front, they moved for us, respect and awe obvious in their eyes.

We made it to the front, peering down below in a meter-wide gap between the edge of the cave mouth and the dropship.

Below us, the Voy moved like ants. They were bringing out larger weapons from a building on the right. Small laser rounds shot up at the dropship, ineffective against the ship's hull.

Something like a rocket was fired at us and this time connected with the dropship. It rattled and groaned. Smoke ascended to the heavens from the dropship's stubby left wing.

"We can't take hits like that. We go now!" Angel yelled. She looked at me. "I get you want to help people, that's cute and all, but if we don't go now, we're all dead."

I looked back at the people pressing in toward the dropship. We needed another minute, two at most.

Spartan was inside trying to find room for all of them.

Rose yelled for people to try and remain calm.

Heart's in the right place, Rose, I thought to myself. *But I don't think anyone's going to be able to be calm right now.*

"She's right, we can't take another hit like that," Preacher said, reaching just inside the dropship to a cable. He attached it to his belt. "Get that alien corpse to Immortal Corp and whoever will listen. Humankind is about to experience an extinction-level event and we're going to need all the help we can get."

"What are you doing?" Angel asked in shock. "No, the mission—"

"Mission's changed," Preacher shouted back, drawing the katana from his back. It glowed a menacing red a moment later. "Get out of here. Warn them!"

I was still in the process of shouting at him not to do it, when he jumped off the cliff wall and started running down the side of the mountain.

The cable gave him just enough resistance to keep him upright and from falling straight down.

And here I was, thinking I had seen it all.

Preacher sprinted down the side of the mountain with his red sword glowing. He was the grim reaper incarnate, but instead of a scythe, he carried the katana in his hands. Death followed with him.

"What the f—" I heard Angel roar in anger before her next words were cut off as another rocket hit the side of the mountain. A second clipped the dropship, sending it into a tremor.

I stared with my mouth open as Preacher reached the ground in record time. He cut himself free from the cable securing his descent then went to work. From this height, his sword looked like a shredder. He waded into the Voy lines toward those with the rockets.

I wanted to go and help and I wanted to watch in wonder at the same time.

"Move," Angel shouted at me as she shoved me toward the dropship.

"We have to go help him," I said back with one foot on the dropship still carrying the Voy carcass across my shoulders. "They'll kill him."

"He made his choice," Angel said.

If I thought she said the words with any kind of levity, I would have argued with her.

Tears splashed down her cheeks. I couldn't tell if they were from anger or frustration, but they sure weren't from sadness. She was pissed.

I boarded the dropship with the last of the prisoners. We were shoved in so tight, it was standing room only.

The dropship was so full, there wasn't even room to close the back ramp.

Rose, Angel, and I were the last to get inside. We stood on the rear ramp.

"Get us out of here," Angel shouted into her earpiece.

As if the dropship itself had heard her, the craft moved away from the cave mouth.

Despite Preacher on the ground trying to give us safe passage, there were simply too many Voy to stop from firing at us. Laser rifle rounds pinged off the hull of the dropship like water. Rockets streaked through the air on either side of us. Apparently, what the Voy made up for in sheer number and physical strength, they lacked in aiming ability. Two more rockets clipped the side of the dropship.

I shoved the Voy carcass into the dropship. I wedged it between a pair of prisoners who understood what I was trying to do and helped me press the corpse deeper into the interior of the cargo area.

I looked down to see Preacher's tiny red blade still swinging as if it had a mind of its own.

Just when it looked like we were about to make it, a rocket slammed into the belly of the dropship, then another into the left wing.

TWELVE

THE ENTIRE SHIP BUCKLED. Smoke poured into the interior of the craft. Escaped prisoners fell out of the rear of the ship, screaming. I grabbed on to a cargo net set into the right wall of the dropship.

Instinct made me reach out with my left hand as someone flew past me out of the dropship. I grabbed on to her hand.

It was Rose.

"Hold on!" Spartan screamed over the speakers set into the inside of the ship. "Hold on!"

It wasn't like he really had to tell me that as the ship lost altitude.

The dropship rolled then spasmed. My feet finally found the ground once more as I pulled Rose deeper into the dropship.

She was shaking, but other than that, safe.

"Th—thanks," Rose managed.

The cargo ramp started to close.

I looked over to where Angel stood beside the control panel. She was bleeding from a wicked cut on her forehead. If the blood in her eyes bothered her, she didn't show it.

Our brush with death cleared out the rear section of the dropship. We had lost a good ten, maybe even twenty escaped prisoners.

I looked out the rear of the ship as the two parts came to a close. I couldn't even see the alien encampment anymore. We were outside the cloaked bubble the Voy used to conceal their base.

It looked like nothing more than the desert and a mountain behind us. Warning lights were flashing inside the dropship. People were crying, others shouting.

"Talk to me," Angel said in the earpiece as she maneuvered her way to the front.

"Do what you can to calm them down," I told Rose as I followed Angel through the ship. "We're going to make it out of this."

Rose nodded.

With so many prisoners just thrown out of the

back of the dropship, moving to the front wasn't that difficult.

When we got to the front, the man I knew as Spartan was using a line of words to curse the likes I had never heard before.

"Son of a monkey's uncle," Spartan said through gritted teeth as he fought the controls.

"How are we doing?" Angel asked, taking a seat in the copilot's chair.

"Oh, you know, just raided an alien compound, watched our leader sacrifice himself, and now we're going to crash land with a dropship full of civilians, the usual," Spartan said without taking his eyes off the window in front of him. "What were you thinking taking the prisoners with us anyway? That wasn't part of the mission."

Angel looked over her shoulder at me.

"Mission changed," she said. "Can we make it?"

"Not to Elysium, if that's what you mean," Spartan grunted as the ship shook again. "We're bleeding fuel and engine one is gone. I can keep her in the air for a few hours at the very most."

"Is there anything within that distance?" I asked, leaning over Angel's seat to get a better view of the map she was bringing up.

"Well, look who it is," Spartan said to me with a

smile that didn't fit the situation. "What's up, wild man? Long time no see."

I couldn't help but like Spartan. We were probably being chased by aliens at the moment, we were definitely going to have to land somewhere in the middle of the far side of Mars, and still he had a grin for me.

"Good to be back," I replied. "Thanks for the assist."

"All in a day's work," Spartan said, turning back to the wheel. The dropship quaked as if it were angry Spartan's attention had been divided for a moment.

"The closest settlement is a Way colony two hours to the north," Angel advised, looking up from the holographic map that popped up above her dashboard. "Can we make it?"

"Oh great, a Way settlement?" Spartan asked, rolling his eyes. "I'd rather go back and take my chances with our four-armed friends."

"Can we make it?" Angel repeated the question. This time, there was a bite in her words.

"Yeah, we'll make it all the way if not most of the way," Spartan said. "Worst case, we have to set down a few kilometers out and trek the rest of the way."

"Any sign of pursuit?" Angel asked, checking the scanners.

"None," Spartan said. "I don't think they care who

knows they're here. Did you see how many of them there were?"

"We need to call this in," I said, remembering the channel X had reminded me of that I'd been unable to use until now. "I have a contact with the Galactic Government who might be able to help."

"I don't think the GG is going to believe any of this," Spartan said. "And even if they did, our communication capability is down, thanks to a well-placed rocket."

"They'll believe us if we can get word out," I reasoned. "We have proof now. We have a corpse."

"Well, that does change things," Spartan acknowledged as his eyebrows rose. "Maybe the Way will have some means to get word out."

"What is the Way?" I asked, unfamiliar with the term. "A private company? Other mercenaries?"

"Worse," Angel warned. "Religion."

"Religion is putting it mildly. It's more like a brainwashing cult," Spartan confirmed. "You're in for it. You'll be reminded of your sins, the way to the light, and all kinds of great things to keep you comforted at night."

"Actually, that doesn't sound too bad compared to being tortured with an insect inside your body," I said, grimacing at the memory. "Kind of sounds like a vacation."

"An insect inside your body?" Spartan asked, taking his eyes off the window in front of him to look at me. "Seriously?"

"They do torture different on other planets, I guess," I said being brought back to the fact that we still knew so little about our new enemies. "You think —you think Preacher—they killed him?"

"For his sake, I hope so," Angel said quietly. "If he did survive, I don't want to think what they're going to do to him."

The cockpit of the dropship grew quiet.

"We'll go back for him," Spartan said as if he were reassuring himself. "We get these people offloaded and word back to Immortal Corp, then we go back for him."

Standing there, I was reminded how badly my body needed fuel. I was past the point of exhaustion, where I just felt numb. Even my thought process seemed to slow.

"You going to make it?" Angel asked, looking at me. "Maybe you should grab some food and rest. We'll be there soon enough."

"Right," I said. "I, uh, I just wanted to say thank

you. Both of you. It's strange for me to talk to you, since my memory is pretty much nonexistent."

"Right, the memory wipe thing," Spartan said, turning in his seat. "I'm Jaxon Aze. Everyone calls me Jax. It's good to meet you again, Daniel. What happened to your memory anyway?"

"I still don't know." I shrugged. "I woke up on the moon with nothing except my name."

"Well, we're glad you're back." Angel turned in her seat and extended a hand. "Angelica Crowley."

I took her hand. Her grip was crushing.

"You two can get some rest and food," Jax relayed as the dropship sputtered for what felt like the hundredth time. "I'll keep us in the air as long as possible. We'll either get there or I'll put us down somewhere safe."

I took one last look out the window to the sun and the rolling dunes of red sand that seemed to extend out as far as the eye could see.

"Food's in the overhead storage area," Angel told me. "I'll be back there in a few. I just have to run a few things by Jax."

I took my cue to leave the cockpit.

The seating area of the dropship was full with prisoners who looked at me with eyes full of hope and fear.

They'd spread out half sitting in the seats and the other half sitting on the floor in the rear of the ship where the empty cargo hold afforded more space for them.

I looked up at the overhead compartments that spanned both sides of the ship. I said a silent prayer there would be enough for everyone and popped open the hatch.

It wasn't a feast, but there were enough dried food bags and protein bars to go around. With this were jugs of water in cartons.

"Hey, is anyone hungry?" I asked.

All eyes turned to me as if I were offering pure gold.

"Well, come on." I pointed to the overhead lockers. "I'm not going to go around handing it to you all."

At once, the inside of the ship was a maelstrom of movement. Hatches were opened, bags were ripped open, and grins spread.

I opened a bag that promised the taste of vegetables and meat. I'd eat dirt at the moment, I was so hungry. To be honest, the food wasn't half bad. I wasn't sure what kind of preservatives and artificial chemicals they had to pump into the food for it to stay good this long, but it did the job.

I stuffed my face, quelling the roaring of my stomach and the pit I felt in my gut.

That same kid who I saw stomping on the dead Voy came over and sat beside me. He didn't say anything. He just opened his own pack of food and started to eat.

"Well, just go ahead and feel free to eat our entire food stock in one meal, why don't you?" Angel commented, exiting the cockpit and taking a look at everyone stuffing their faces. "This was supposed to last us."

"You can take it away from them if you want." I shrugged. "That's on you."

The little boy beside me moved his pack of food to the side as if he could hide it from Angel.

"Yeah, we both know I'm not going to do that," Angel said with an eye roll. She went over to an open overhead storage locker and grabbed a carton of water.

"What's the word?" Rose asked, coming over to us with a protein bar in her palm. "We going to make it to Elysium like this?"

"Not exactly," Angel hedged. "We'll make it as far as a settlement to the north. We'll use their radio to call in for help."

"What settlement?" an older man asked. It was hard to tell, but it looked by what remained of his clothing they had been nice and finely made at some point long ago. "I need to get to Elysium. If not

Elysium, at least Athens or Delphi. I have money. I mean, not money with me, but I can pay you well once we arrive."

"Good for you," Angel deadpanned, not amused in the least. "The ship's not going to make it much farther. We'll get to the settlement then radio for help. That's the plan."

The man huffed. Now free from being treated like an animal, he seemed to have regained some of his former airs of importance.

"And what is this settlement where we will be landing?" he demanded.

"It's a Way colony," Angel answered. "It's the only thing this far out here. I mean, besides the aliens."

"The Way?" someone else asked. "Aren't they a cult? You can't take us there."

A few more murmurs of agreement echoed inside the dropship.

"Great," Angel snapped, draining her carton of water. "I don't see any bars on the back cargo bay doors. If you want out, then be my guest. Throw yourself out. I'm not keeping you here. If you don't want to come then don't."

The room inside the ship quieted. It was clear no one was going to jump out of the moving dropship.

"How very human of everyone," Rose muttered.

"Save them, you'd think they'd be nothing but grateful but once elevated from the station of an animal entitlement starts settling in."

"We're not out of this yet," Angel said, raising an eyebrow. "We're not out of this yet."

THIRTEEN

I ATE AS MUCH as I could from the bagged meals, going through a few that tasted like man made food more than any kind of natural ingredients I had ever put into my mouth. It did the job.

I leaned back in my chair, giving in to my body's fatigue. My dreams were nightmares of the Voy, torture, and Preacher.

I woke in a cold sweat, breathing hard. My mind went back to Preacher. If he had survived, then what were they doing to him now? I couldn't leave him like that. We couldn't leave him like that. Not after what he had done to save us.

"Are you all right?" X asked from the circular disc in my pocket. "You were muttering in your sleep."

"Just nightmares," I answered. "We have to go back for him. I can't imagine what they're doing to him."

"We will," X said. "But not with a damaged drop-ship full of half-starved prisoners. We get these people to safety then go back with a plan to free him. Daniel, I'm not sure the Voy can be beat. I saw their numbers and the thousands of warriors they have growing in the mountain. It'll take an army of our own to do it."

"Then we'll get an army of our own," I said, straightening in my seat. "We'll get an army, even if it means going to the Galactic Government for help."

"Even if it means siding with Immortal Corp?" X asked.

"The last thing I want to do is partner with them, but like Preacher said, this goes past what I want or need, this goes to the very survival of the human race," I said. "We need to get you back inside my head too."

"Awww, do you miss me?" X asked.

"Don't get all mushy on me," I said. "But yeah, it feels off not having you with me."

"I agree," X confessed. "With a few tools, I can instruct you on how to transfer my data from this piece of alien tech and reinsert me into your neck."

"Good," I said, thinking to one of the many questions I still had about the Voy. "X, while you were plugged into their system, did you find out where the Voy came from? Who they are?"

"I saw it in a flash," X answered. "There was so much data to sift through while I was inside their network. They're a political race that explores galaxies for resources. They were light years away from Earth when we set off one of their early warning alarms. Our move from Earth to the moon put us on their radar. When humanity moved from the moon to Mars, they came looking."

"We waved a flag letting them know we were a somewhat intelligent species and might have resources they wanted," I concluded, finishing X's story. "So, what? They came to Mars to abduct and experiment on humans until they grew an army?"

"Pretty much." X sighed wearily. "There are so many of them, Daniel. You were able to fight them because you're stronger and faster than other humans. One on one against a Voy, most humans wouldn't have a chance. The way they grow their soldiers as well. It means an infinite supply."

"An infinite supply unless we destroy that lab they have where they grow them," I corrected. "If we were going to take them on, what size force would we need?"

"You'd need everyone." X paused to correct herself.

"You'd need the combined efforts of the Galactic Government and more than half of the smaller companies sending their forces to help."

"The war for mankind," I said, shaking my head. I was still trying to believe it. "Anything else you can tell me? Anything else you picked up while you were inside?"

"Only that this is just a normal routine for the Voy," X said. "I mean, this is just a scouting party who was sent out to grow the army and run experiments. They have many other parties like this who are spread out exploring the universe from their home planet."

"Great," I said. "Hopefully, defeating the Voy on Mars will be enough to tell the rest of them to stay away."

"I believe it will be," X agreed. "The Voy are concerned with protecting their resources and investing wisely. If humankind shows the Voy they are able to fight, then it won't make sense for the Voy empire to throw more of its soldiers or resources against us."

"Let's hope so," I said. "I think—"

I was interrupted by Jax's voice over the speakers. "Ladies, gentlemen, Angel, we're running on fumes at the moment and still a few kilometers out from the Way settlement. I'm going to have to put her down on the sand. Sit down and buckle in. It's about to get bumpy."

I looked around at the wide-eyed group in the dropship. Although it wasn't cramped anymore, we had a full house. Those near seats strapped in while the others in the cargo bay took seats on the floor and held on to whatever they could.

I moved out of my seat and gave it to a small girl. The girl didn't look like she could have been much older than Sam's daughter back in the Badlands.

I decided to remain standing in the cargo bay. I grabbed on to one of the nets on the side of the wall.

The dropship whined and creaked as my gut lifted into my throat. We were losing altitude and everyone in the dropship could feel it. Moans and grunts escaped their throats.

I got that excited anticipation of touching down to the ground. The one that grabs you when you can't see exactly how close you are to the floor but you'd bet your life you'd be hitting it at any moment.

The windows along the sides of the dropship cabin were open, for the most part letting in the last rays of the setting sun. Mars' twin moons could be seen ready to take over their dominant roles in the sky, but that wasn't my focus at the moment.

We dropped again and again until the sand dunes on either side of the window rose up to touch us.

"We're going in too fast," X warned from my pocket.

"Hold on to your butts!" Jax yelled via the speakers.

The dropship touched down, skidding along the sand. The entire ship quaked and rocked. People screamed and shouted inside. Luckily, everyone remained secured and in their place, holding on to one another for support.

The lights blinked off and on inside the craft. An acrid smell of smoke and something burning touched my nostrils then moved to the back of my throat. I could practically taste it.

We kept skidding for what felt like an entire kilometer before the ship came to a stop.

The rear doors of the dropship opened as Jax and Angel came out of the cockpit.

"Please hold your applause," Jax said with a wide grin on his bearded face. "I know that was some amazing flying, but I'm humble, really."

Everyone looked at him, some dumbfounded, trying to figure out if he was being serious or not, others grateful to be alive.

"We're still a few kilometers out from the settlement," Angel relayed, motioning me over. "We'll have to walk the rest of the way. Those of you unable to make the trip are welcome to stay here. There's food and water. We'll get to the settlement tonight and radio in to the closest major city for aid."

I walked over to Angel as she informed everyone what would be happening. Those inside the dropship began talking amongst themselves about who would stay and who wanted to make the trip.

"We've got to do something with our alien friend," Angel said, looking at the corpse of the Voy I had carried aboard. It was tangled in the cargo net so as not to move around the ship. It was already beginning to smell.

"There's a cooler it could probably fit inside," Jax mused, tapping a finger to his chin. "We can use the shuttle bot to take it with us."

"And when the settlers of the Way ask what's in the box?" Angel asked. "We tell them what?"

"Tell them it's nothing to worry about," Jax said with a shrug. "We say we have to keep it closed. It's a human organ we're transferring or something."

"I agree with Jax on everything besides the human organ part," I said with a disapproving frown. "I think that'll raise too many questions. We'll figure it out if they ask. Maybe we say we're just transporting something for our boss. That we don't even know what it is."

"All right," Angel said. "Let's get a move on. It's already getting dark. The faster we get to the settlement, the faster we radio for help and go back for Preacher. I don't want to think what they're doing to him."

I nodded grimly.

Jax and I moved the stinking alien corpse to a cold chest large enough to fit the body inside if we folded the knees to the chest and tucked the head. The Voy looked like it was resting in the fetal position.

"I can't believe it," Jax remarked as we worked on putting the alien inside the cooler. "I can't believe it. Like, I always figured they were out there. The universe is too big a place to think that humans are the only ones. Still, seeing it is something totally different."

"They're real, and apparently, they want to enslave all of us," I cautioned, closing the cold chest. "They have an army."

"We'll be alright," Jax said, looking at me with a wink. "We have the famous Daniel Hunt back."

"Right," I said. "I'm still piecing together what that means."

"Daniel." Jax's tone took a serious turn. "I—about

Amber—I'm not good with this kind of stuff, but she was like a sister to me. When I found out what Echo did, we tore into each other. I almost left Immortal Corp, but they had a mission for me to go on that I couldn't refuse. I'm sorry."

"Me too," I said. I felt like there was more to be exchanged in that conversation, but neither of us knew how to navigate the rest of our feelings.

"You two going to stare longingly into each other's eyes or what?" Angel asked in a huff. "I'm trying to get this show on the road. Load the cold chest on the shuttle bot and let's get a move on."

Jax and I obeyed, maneuvering the heavy chest onto the square piece of metal that hovered just above the floor when activated. Jax synced the tech to a screen on the back of his left vambrace.

"All right, we're heading out," Rose called. She had taken lead on helping to sort the newly liberated prisoners. It seemed half their number were going to stay behind while the other half joined us on the trek to the settlement.

Goodbyes and waves were made as those too weak or injured remained behind.

"We'll send help," Rose promised them. "Give us a day or two, and we'll be back with help."

Angel and I took the lead while Jax brought up the rear with the shuttle bot.

Darkness had come. With it, a world bathed in the silver glow of the stars and moons overhead. We walked in silence for the most part, each of us lost to his or her own thoughts.

It was amazing what food and rest could do for you. I felt rejuvenated. With a hot shower, I'd be as good as new. I needed to find a way to get X back connected with me. Like she said, as long as the Way settlement had any kind of tools, we'd be able to make that happen soon enough.

I was wondering how Immortal Corp, the Galactic Government, and everyone else was going to take the news of an impending alien invasion, when Angel stopped in her tracks.

"What's wrong?" I asked, looking into her eyes for answers. I followed her gaze. "What's going o—"

I stopped myself from finishing the question. Despite the darkness, I could see a plume of smoke in the distance. The Way settlement was on fire.

FOURTEEN

"WE'VE GOT A SITUATION," Angel said in the comm unit she wore on her right ear. "Fire in the distance."

While Angel and Jax coordinated a plan, I ran to a dune on the left to get a better vantage point. It was useless since the night was too dark. All I could confirm was that there was in fact some kind of structure burning in the distance. Yellow and orange flames licked at a building I couldn't make out.

Rose and the others were beginning to see it too as questions no one had answers for ripped through those gathered.

"What is it?" someone asked.

"More trouble?" another voice added.

"Is there a fire?" a third person inquired.

"Let's go," Angel called up to me. "The settlement

is our best shot at calling for help. Whatever issue they have has become our issue now."

Jax caught up to the front of the group with the shuttle bot carrying the cold chest close behind. He handed off the piece of equipment to Rose with orders to follow at their own pace.

Just like that, we were off.

Angel, Jax, and I sprinted across the Mars sand dunes like wolves on the hunt. The smell of smoke was heavy in the air, and as I ran with my brother and sister, I couldn't help but feel a tingle of excitement.

Is this normal? I wondered to myself. *Do normal people get excited at the idea of danger?*

I didn't have an answer for that question, but I did know I enjoyed the wind in my hair. A sense of adventure touched my heart as Angel ran on my right and Jax my left. For a brief moment, I was given an insight to how things might have been before.

Maybe this had been like those missions Immortal Corp sent us on. Mercenaries trusting each other with their lives, each warrior more menacing than the next. We were invincible together.

The burning settlement took on shape as we crossed the desert landscape at full-out sprints. I was happy to see that only one building inside the outer walls was actually in flames.

Shouts and orders were being exchanged inside the settlement walls as people tried to put the fire out.

Entering the wide open front gates, I got my first good look at the settlement. Stone pillars no more than a half-meter wide rose up three stories like giant spikes from the ground. This formed a wall around the inside of the settlement that seemed unnecessary, since the gates to the compound were open.

Angel, Jax, and I came to a halt just inside the gates. The settlement was small with not more than a dozen buildings sprawled inside the walls. They were all made of the same stone as the perimeter wall. White bricks had been carved out of rock to make the single story structures inside. Slanted roofs with chimneys and vents lay on top of the walls.

At the moment, at least eighty people all dressed in white were working to put out the fire, which had consumed a building in the north section inside the walls.

It seemed as though we were a second too late to help. The settlers had canisters that sprayed some kind of thick, white foam. Right now, they had surrounded the building and were in the process of putting out the flame.

We ran forward anyway. The inside of the settlement was bathed in the light of giant lamp posts that shone down on all of us. They were strategically placed to bring light to every corner of the settlement.

I saw an older man shouting orders to the people. I ran over to him.

"We can help," I said, not bothering with introductions at the moment. "I can help."

"Yes, I've been expecting you three," the man said, looking at me without batting an eye. "There are foam sprayers over by that lamp post to the right. With your abilities, would you mind getting closer to the fire and battling it from inside the building?"

I did a double take, looking at Angel and Jax for help.

They shrugged.

I was sure I had never seen the man before. He was bald and clean-shaven. His sun beaten skin was wrinkled. He wore a white robe like many of the others inside the walls. On his left shoulder was the sigil of a rising or setting sun. I couldn't be sure which.

"Can you do that?" the man asked me. "Are you okay?"

"Yeah, sure," I said, still thrown off by his greeting. It was like he was expecting us and he had referenced our abilities. How could he have known?

"Well, that's not creepy at all," Jax muttered, jogging over and grabbing one of the yellow foam canisters. "How could he have known we have healing abilities?"

"This place freaks me out," Angel said, also grabbing a canister and turning toward the building. "Let's take care of his fire then radio for help ASAP. The sooner we get out of here, the better."

I didn't disagree with either of them. Not only did the man not seem fazed to see us at all, but the other settlers seemed to expect us as well. They nodded to us with welcome smiles and shining eyes.

The building that was on fire was a square structure made from white rock. The rocks of course weren't burning but instead whatever was inside the building as well as the roof.

Black smoke billowed from the open door and windows. Someone came over with three masks for us to wear. I accepted mine, placing it over my face. There was a clear plastic screen to see out of. The bottom from my nose to my chin was covered in a ventilator that would cycle out the smoke and allow me to breathe clean air.

Equipped with the masks and our foam canisters, we waded into the building. I had no idea what started the fire or what had been in the room before, but it was reduced to a pile of smoldering furniture and tech at the moment. The roof was also on fire, although those outside had taken the flames' intense inferno down to a manageable level.

We went to work using the canisters of foam on the fire while ignoring the intense heat. Sure the warmth wasn't fun, but there was a sense of relief knowing that a little fire wasn't going to hurt.

Compared to being torched by that mutie back in the city of Cecile, putting out this fire seemed like a piece of cake. I think Jax was actually whistling while he worked.

In a matter of minutes, the flames that did exist were sputtering. The smoke escaped through sections of the roof that had burned down.

I stepped outside, followed by Angel and Jax.

"Praise be to the Lord of the Heavens." The man who had welcomed us before came to us, slapping his hands in front of his chest. "My name is Enoch and these are the followers of the Way. We are so happy to see you, Daniel, Angelica, and Jaxon."

I looked at Angel and Jax to make sure I wasn't the only one weirded out by how much Enoch knew about us.

"Listen, padre," Angel started, removing her mask and letting it drop to the ground. "I'm not sure how you know anything about us, but we need to use your radio. We have a lot of issues of our own at the moment."

"Of course, of course, " Enoch said with a shrug. "But you just put out the flames in the radio room."

"Of course we did." Jax snickered, taking off his mask and laughing out loud. "Of course the only building on fire would be the one holding the radio equipment."

"You have to have some other means of communication," I said, ignoring Jax. "How do you get supplies?"

"Oh, we do," Enoch said. "We have supplies come in every week from Elysium. "The next shipment is set to arrive in two days."

"What about transport from here back to Elysium?" Angel asked. "Anything will do. A Raptor, dropship or--hey what about going back for the Raptor you and Preacher came in on?"

"The one in Voy infested territory?" I asked.

"I can take that option off the board," X chimed in. "The Voy found it."

"Well you have to have something here," Angel turned back to Enoch. "I mean..."

Her voice trailed off as Enoch looked at her, amused.

"You don't have any way to get out of here, do you?" Angel said.

"Just the two legs the good Lord gave me," Enoch answered. "I understand your need to get help and word out, but trust me. Everything happens for a reason. You were meant to be here as much as you are meant to stay for these two days. In two days, our regular supplies will come in. You can use their radio. I'm sure they'll even give you a ride back to the city."

"How did you know our names?" I wondered, already accepting we were stuck there for two days and moving on. "You knew our names and that we could help with the fire using our abilities."

"The good Lord sent your faces and names to me in a dream," Enoch explained as matter-of-factly as if he were reading from a book. "He said you would be suited to help us. Especially suited, I might add."

"Great," Jax said, rolling his eyes. "Did he happen to say we would be hungry when we arrived? Or that we would be coming with forty recently freed prisoners as well?"

"The Lord works in mysterious ways, my friend," Enoch said, opening his arms to take in the compound. "We don't have much in the way of food, but what we have is yours. You and all who travel with you are welcome here."

"Sister Monroe?" Enoch called, motioning to a pretty woman with a white ribbon in her hair. "Will you please take a few of the others and greet our guests coming in through the front gate? Jax said they will be on their way."

"Of course." Sister Monroe looked at me sideways then blushed when she saw I caught her looking. She started gathering a few of the others to greet Rose and the rest of our group.

"You have to forgive us," Enoch said as I took in a few more of the white-robed men and women gawking at us. "It's not every day we get visitors from the outside. We're a bit secluded out here in the untamed side of Mars."

"You have no idea," Jax said with a heavy sigh. "You're not as secluded as you think—"

Angel planted an elbow in his ribs before he could say more.

"Why don't we go see the rest of the travelers in," Angel suggested , staring daggers at Jax. "Rose has that chest she needs help with."

"You didn't have to hit me so hard," Jax said, rubbing his ribs. "You've got some bony elbows on you, lady."

Angel and Jax moved on to secure the cold chest. I found myself alone with Enoch.

"How did the fire start anyway?" I asked. What I really wanted to do was dig deeper into exactly how he knew our names and that we had these certain abilities, but something told me he was just going to give me the same answer. As far as I was concerned, that was no real answer at all.

"Oh, the Hessian started it," Enoch said as if I were supposed to know exactly what that meant. "Don't worry, we've locked her up for everyone's wellbeing. She won't be causing any more trouble."

FIFTEEN

"HESSIAN?" I repeated. I was sure I had never heard the word before. "Who's that?"

"I'll show you," Enoch said, waving me over to walk beside him. "We welcomed her in when she arrived just like we would any other traveler. Our gates are always open. She stayed with us a few days. We caught her trying to steal from our radio room. When she was caught, she started the fire in an attempt to escape. We caught her anyway. She'll be taken with the supply craft when it makes for Elysium and handed over to the Galactic Government."

We made our way between the buildings constructed of white stone. The layout of the settlement was simple and spread out. No statues or fountains like Elysium. I had to admit there was a sense of peace here, as if life took on a slower cadence from the outside world.

Toward the rear of the settlement, we came to three metal holes in the ground. Each hole was secured with a steel circular grate large enough for someone to fit inside. Through the bars of the grate, I could make out a form below. It was too dark now to see much else.

"I'll leave you to it," Enoch said with a knowing smile. He placed a hand on my shoulder. "I'm glad our paths have crossed in this world, Daniel."

He turned to go, then as an afterthought, looked over his shoulder.

"Daniel, do you know what your name means?" Enoch asked.

"I have no idea," I said, still trying to figure out what I was supposed to be doing here with this Hessian.

"It means God is my judge," Enoch said as if that was supposed to answer some question I had. He turned to go again.

"Wait, what exactly did you want me to do here?" I asked, half turning to go with him.

"Just talk to her," Enoch said. "You'll see."

He left me there with my mouth open. I had half a mind just to walk away right there and then. I had no desire to talk to this Hessian. If anything, I needed to go meet up with Angel and Jax.

"He does that," a voice said from under the steel grate. It was a young girl's voice. Not a child, but someone who couldn't yet be out of their late teenage years. "I didn't mean to burn that place down. It was knee-jerk reaction when I was trying to get out of there."

"Yeah, right," I scoffed, not believing her for a minute. "I bet it was a mistake trying to steal their stuff too."

"No, no, I did that on purpose," she said with a heavy sigh. "Hey, you don't have any stim on you, do you?"

I was familiar with the drug. When I worked as a gladiator on the moon, I had thrown out my fair share of users. I had seen firsthand what the stuff could do. It rotted its consumers from the inside out.

"No, and you should stay away from that stuff," I admonished. "Long-time users are nothing more than walking corpses."

"Oh great, you going to teach me about the Way as well?" she asked. "I felt like I was getting tortured when they put me in here and started sharing their cult mumbo jumbo with me."

"Nope, not really my style," I said. "Hey, what's a Hessian anyway?"

"You aren't from Mars, are you?" she asked.

"Not that I know of," I said honestly.

"You've never heard of the Hessians?" she asked again, which was pointless because I had just asked. "We're a thieves' gang out of Athens. Sure you don't have any stim on you? I'm kind of freaking out here. I just need a quick fix, something to hold me over."

I could hear the near panic in her voice. Detox was going to be more than rough for her. It was going to be one hell of a night in her hole.

"Nothing," I said without remorse. "You'll have to clean up if you're going to make it through the night."

"Come on, but you can get some for me, right?" she whined as she sensed a close to the conversation and her without her fix. "I mean, someone here has to have something. Maybe someone you came with. Come on, Daniel, you have to help me out here."

"Maybe I am helping you," I said. I thought about the withdrawals the human body would go through without stim. It wasn't pretty. I thought about my own demons from the past I had to face. "When the cold sweats and nightmares come for you, don't be afraid to scream out. I won't judge you. There's freedom in it."

"What!?" she said. "What kind of help is that? Thanks for nothing, weirdo!"

I walked away from the hole, wondering why Enoch had wanted me to talk to her. Was it some kind of test? Was it for her or for me?

By the time I reached the front gates again, the rest of the survivors from the Voy prison camp were trickling in.

Enoch and his settlers came to them with water and food, clean clothes, and offers to bathe. It was only a matter of time before the recently freed prisoners related their entire story to Enoch and his people.

Soon we'd have our hands full of questions about the Voy. Rose, Jax, Angel, and I were shown to a small simple building with bunk beds fitted with clean white sheets. The space didn't allow for much more than the beds and a small washroom to the side.

For light, there was a pair of lanterns that burned bright with some kind of white energy.

"Where are we going to put this thing?" Jax asked, motioning to the cold chest in the small room. "I don't want to sleep by it."

"Such a baby," Angel said, rolling her eyes. "Here."

Angel shoved the cold chest under the bottom bunk she shared with Jax.

"Questions are going to come at any moment,"

Rose said, rubbing her tired eyes. "The other freed prisoners are already talking. The people here will want answers."

I ran my tongue around the inside of my mouth.

"We should tell them the truth," I decided.

"What truth?" Angel asked. "That they're a hard day's ride from an invisible alien incursion? How do you think they're going to handle that?"

"Daniel's right," Jax interrupted. "They should have the chance to clear out. When the Voy are ready to make their move, this place has no chance of stopping them. They'll be slaughtered."

"I mean, yeah, go ahead. Be my guest," Angel said with a shrug. "I'm still trying to understand it all myself. I don't know how I'm going to explain it to someone else."

A gentle knock came at our door.

Rose went over to open it.

Enoch stood there with Sister Monroe. The former hadn't lost his welcoming demeanor, the latter looked like his polar opposite. The blood gone from her face. She looked like she'd seen a ghost.

"Might we have a few moments of your time?" Enoch asked. "It seems those you travel with bring some disturbing news with them."

"I'm going to go shower," Angel said with a wave. "Good luck with this one."

Angel walked to the adjoining wash area and closed the door.

I told them everything I knew, with Rose peppering in details as I went. Jax remained silent for the most part. I told them of being captured, our escape, and that we had no idea what happened to Preacher, but we were going back for him.

Enoch listened intently. I thought Sister Monroe was going to have a panic attack at any second. Her eyes bulged out of her head as if she couldn't believe the words coming out of my mouth. I didn't blame her. I could barely believe the words coming out of my own mouth.

"We're going to get word out, rearm, and go back for Preacher," I finished. "But you should gather your people and head back with the supply craft that's coming. It's not safe for you out here anymore."

A long silence passed as Enoch and Sister Monroe digested the information.

"Is that what you have in there?" Enoch asked, motioning with his chin to the cold chest. "You brought one of them with you?"

"Proof," Jax said. "No one besides Immortal Corp thought this could happen. When we try and get help from the Galactic Government or other factions, we'll need more than a crazy story to tell them. Seeing is believing, right?"

"May I?" Enoch asked. "It's not that I don't believe you. To the contrary, your tale is too amazing not to be true. It's just that I'd like to see it."

"Sure," I said.

Rose went over to the cold chest and kicked open the lid.

Tendrils of cold wafted up into the room. A thin layer of frost had covered the alien. Its four arms were crossed over itself as if it were trying to fend off the cold. All six of its eyes were closed as if it were asleep.

Sister Monroe gave out a short scream then clamped her hand to her mouth. She looked unsteady on her feet. She sat down hard on the lower bed of one of the bunks.

Enoch swallowed hard. He shook his head as if he too were having some kind of mental break.

"I don't—I don't know what to say," Enoch stammered. "How can this be possible?"

"I don't know, but what I do know is that this settlement is no longer safe," Rose said. She spoke softly. "You need to get to the safety of one of the cities. Even that might not be far enough away when the fighting starts. We're not sure if it will begin next week, next month, or next year, but war is coming. You can't stay here anymore."

Enoch nodded dumbly.

"Take a minute to come to grips with this new reality and then come up with a plan," Jax told Enoch and Sister Monroe. "I'm not sure what the Way's stance on aliens is, but I imagine that you can do more good alive than dead. You'll want to clear out of here when the supply craft comes like Daniel suggested."

Enoch nodded along with Jax's words.

"We need to tell the others," Enoch said, leaving the building. "For whatever reason the Lord has chosen to allow this to happen, I rest assured it is part of his plan. And I am grateful for all of you coming to warn us."

"We do what we can," Jax said.

Enoch and Sister Monroe left.

"I almost feel sorry for them. Dropping a bomb on them like that, I mean," Rose said with a weary sigh. "But they have to know. Everyone has to know."

The rest of the night was short lived. We took turns in the shower then fell asleep for the night. In the middle of the night, I woke to hear Hessian girl screaming away her past sins.

Atta girl, I thought to myself as I fell back to sleep. *Let it out. You let your demons go.*

SIXTEEN

THE NEXT MORNING, the settlement was alive with the tense anxiety of knowing we weren't alone in the universe. It was strange how panic could set in and even fracture normally grounded people.

After a hot breakfast in a long building with benches, I was on the way back to my designated housing unit. The idea was to pass the day getting as much rest as possible and the following morning would see the supply craft to the settlement. Once that happened, there was no telling when the next time was I'd get food or sleep.

My plan was to spread the word about the aliens to those in power then leave it to them to do the rest. We needed to reequip and go back in to find Preacher. We could do it with a small team or even a larger assault squad. It didn't matter to me.

The sun was still fighting the cold in the morning air when I arrived back at my designated building. A group of men and woman in white robes had gathered there.

Scowls written across their faces told me they weren't there for a social call.

Sister Monroe had her back to the door, trying to calm them.

"They only brought the news to us," Sister Monroe was saying above the hubbub of the crowd. "They had no hand in the aliens coming to Mars."

"We want them out!" a woman shouted.

"They can't stay here anymore," another voice from the crowd yelled.

"What's going on here?" I asked, pushing my way to the front door. I stood next to Sister Monroe, who looked grateful for my arrival.

"We want you out of here!" a burly man with a thick beard and bald head said, stepping forward. "You bring nothing but bad news and hungry mouths with you. Normally, that would be fine, but now you want us to leave our home? We already left everything we had in the cities for a life here."

"I don't want you to do anything," I said, looking

the man straight in the eye. "You can stay here and burn for all I care. But you need to know the truth. The aliens are here. When they attack Mars, you'll be the first to go. They'll kill most of you and enslave the rest."

I got it. They were scared, and for most, fear turns to anger.

"We want you to go," the man yelled in my face. He bunched up his fists. "You and everyone who came with you. Go back to your cities and leave us be."

"That is not the consensus of the elders, Eli," Sister Monroe said back to the man. "They are our guests and bring us a warning. We should be thanking them."

"Thanking them?" Eli spat. "I want them gone. Now!"

"You look like you want to hit me," I told Eli, stepping up to him. "I get it. Really I do. You have a family, friends, an entire way of life you're about to lose. You gave up everything for this and now everything you rebuilt is about to be taken away. You're frustrated, angry, and scared. Those are all human emotions. It's good to have an outlet. Go ahead, hit me."

Eli looked at me, confused. The crowd quieted.

Even Sister Monroe stopped trying to calm them. She turned to me, mouth open as if she had never heard anyone welcome violence before.

"Go ahead, hit me and keep on hitting me until you feel better," I told Eli. "Don't back down now. You were doing good. Come on. Where's all the righteous wrath you just had a moment ago?"

Eli glanced at me, then Sister Monroe, and then back at me. He still looked angry, but now that same anger was laced with confusion and frustration.

I needed to push him over the edge. It would help quell the chaos for the time being. We only had to make it until tomorrow when the resupply craft came in.

"Come on, Eli!" I lifted my voice and shoved him, while being sure to hold back. I didn't want to knock him to the ground. "I'm the one you're angry at. I'm the one that came in with the news and ruined your life. Come on, where's all that talk now? Are you all bark and no bite? Come on, come on, hit me!"

Eli wrapped his hands into fists and struck me across the jaw.

"There you go, just like that, now come on," I coaxed him, wiping away the blood from my split lip. "Come on, let's go, keep it coming, brother."

Eli had the taste of what letting his anger out in the form of violence felt like now. He wanted more. I could see it in his face. He rained blows down on me from both his fists. His attacks were clumsy at best. Had this been a real fight, I would have blocked all of them and put him down in seconds. But this wasn't about me. It was about him.

I covered up, absorbing the blows and protecting my face with my hands and arms. Eli hit hard but not very effectively. He got in another good shot or two, but that was about it.

Like most fighters not conditioned for a real battle, he began to tire after a dozen blows or so. Moving all that weight in his arms was wearing him down faster than he thought.

"There we go! Come on, Eli, come on!" I said, urging him on when I saw him getting gassed. "A few more. You got a few more good hits in you, don't stop now."

Eli was sweating, air coming into his lungs in long hard pulls.

I could hear the aghast whispers in the crowd as his friends looked on, mortified by the violence taking place in front of them.

Eli finally took a step back, his arms hanging by his side. I felt for him. I knew what it was like to be that tired.

I lowered my hands. The metallic taste of blood filled my mouth. The cut on my lip was already healing. My left eye was a bit swollen, but that too was already starting to heal up.

"Feel better?" I asked, Eli.

The large man's shoulders dropped. He looked at me with tears in his eyes. "I'm so—I'm sorry."

"You'll be alright," I said, spitting a wad of blood to my right. "You get to be angry and frustrated, but only for a time. You've got to move on. Live in the past, die in the present. Trust me."

Eli nodded slowly.

The tense moment broken, Eli and his band of white-robed followers slowly dispersed with their heads down. It was as if I had shamed them all just by letting Eli take a few swings at me.

"I'm so sorry," Sister Monroe offered with a wince. "It's usually not like that around here. Violence of any kind isn't allowed in the settlement. Eli will be dealt with—"

"It's okay," I told her. "They've been through a lot and they're going to be through a lot more before this is all over. If a few clumsy blows diffused this situation instead of bloodshed, then I'm all for that. I've seen too much blood spilled for no good reason. I'll be the cause of a lot more blood spilled before this is all over."

Sister Monroe took a step back, eyeing the MK II at my hip.

"Do you have some kind of workshop or shed here?" I asked, remembering X was still in the circular alien tech.

"We do, I can show you," Sister Monroe said, swallowing hard. It was clear she had been disturbed by the acts of violence that had just taken place beside her.

I followed her to the north side of the compound where the building had burned the night before. She led me to an identical building to the left and opened the door.

"In here," she said. "You're free to use anything we have."

She hesitated for a moment longer, studying my face.

"You—you could have hurt him, couldn't you?" she asked. "I mean, really hurt him. You could have killed him and I don't mean with the weapon at your side. I mean with your hands. Why—why did you let him do that to you?"

"He needed it more than I did," I told her. "You want to ask another question, though. Go ahead."

She took a moment to gather her thoughts. She

licked her full lips moving in to touch my face. My own lip and eye had already healed.

She touched my lip and ran smooth fingers over the eye that had been swollen only a few moments before. It was fine now.

"Enoch said you'd be different, but I don't know how this is possible." Sister Monroe's hand fell to the side of my cheek.

"I'm not what you're looking for," I told her, removing her hand from my face and letting it fall by her side.

"How do you know?" Sister Monroe asked with her eyes lowered to the ground.

"Because my past is one of death, and there's a lot more killing that's going to take place before my story is over," I told her. "Thank you for showing me the workshop."

I didn't wait for her to argue or say something else that would only prolong the inevitable.

I walked into the shop, taking stock of the room. There were worktables along the wall as well as cages of tools and equipment. I was surprised by how well-equipped the settlement's workshop really was. I expected them to have something, but not an entire store full of tools.

"X," I said, taking out the alien disc. "I'm just

going to be honest with you here. I have no idea what I'm doing."

"Well, you don't want a relationship right now, so you did the right thing," X answered. "You could have let her down a little easier, though."

"I didn't mean with my love life...actually, I have no idea about that either," I said with a grin. "You a love doctor too?"

"I'm just here for you, in whatever capacity you need," X said quietly. "But enough of this bonding. Get me back in your head."

"I'm trying." I laughed out loud. "What am I looking for?"

Over the next few hours, X walked me through the process of transferring her data to a chip and once again implanting her in my neck.

The alien disc was nothing more than a communication device that was now dead. Either the Voy had turned it off or we were out of range from any of their transmissions.

Once that was completed, I attached the chip to a sizable needle-like anchor that would need to be shoved into the space right behind my right ear. X seemed hesitant.

"You might want to get Jax or Angel for this next part," X informed me. "The spot has to be specific and you'll need to really press hard to implant the anchor."

"I got it," I said. "I've done it before."

"Yes, but the anchor you used was small the first time, this one—"

I slammed the needle point into the area right behind my ear.

X was right. Of course she was right. I worked my jaw up and down, trying to deal with the pain. A metallic taste flooded my mouth.

I blinked a few times, gathering myself.

"Wow, that was different," I mumbled. "X—X did it work?"

"Yes, yes, it's good to see again," X said inside my head. "You should really listen to me, though. You're going to have a headache for a while now and taste metal for the next day."

"I'll make a note of that," I said, blinking a few more times.

Weapons fire from inside the settlement tore me from what I was going to say next. It was as though the sky opened up and a thunderstorm raged just outside the door.

What now? I thought to myself. In all honesty, I didn't even want to know.

SEVENTEEN

I RIPPED THE DOOR OPEN, practically taking it off its hinges. I raced outside, my MK II already in hand. I had been in the workshop longer than I thought. The midday meal was already over. My stomach reminded me of that. The sun was going down.

I scanned the area as people in the settlement ran in fear. Others looked at me for direction, still others shouted questions.

The sounds of the weapon being discharged reached my ears again. It was coming from somewhere near the front gates. I skidded to a stop where a crowd was gathering in front of the open gates.

Angel was there with her smoking blaster. The silencer she normally used was removed. At her feet, the corpse of a Voy lay spasming.

Settlers screamed when they saw the thing. By now, they had all heard we weren't alone in the universe, but seeing was something much different.

The dead Voy meant so much more for them than a simple alien presence in the universe. It was enough to challenge everything they believed at their very core.

Jax and I reached Angel at the same time.

"They're coming," Angel said. "I should have known they wouldn't just let us go. I found this one scouting out the perimeter of the settlement. When it tried to sneak in, I let him have it."

Jax kneeled down with pursed lips. "If this is a scout, the others won't be far behind."

"What are you saying?" The voice was Eli's. "More...more of them are coming here?"

"They'll probably attack tonight," I answered.

"How—how do you know that?" Eli sputtered.

"Because that's what I'd do," I told him.

Enoch and Sister Monroe appeared a moment later. Both of them looked from the dead alien to me and then back again.

"When did you say that supply ship is coming?" Jax asked, looking up from the dead alien.

"Tomorrow—tomorrow morning," Enoch said.

For the first time since I had met the man, he looked disturbed. Thus far, he had taken the news of aliens like a champ. This was too much for him and I didn't blame him.

"We have to make it through the night," Angel thought out loud.

"Should we try and leave?" Rose asked. The hard woman didn't sound scared in the least. After what she had been through, I doubted very many things were going to scare her now.

"And go where?" I asked. "Out in the open, we'll be easy targets for them to pick off. Our highest chance at survival is to fortify this place as best we can and weather the night."

"The freed prisoners who stayed behind in the dropship?" Rose asked.

I shook my head.

"If they're already here, you can bet they found the dropship," Angel said. "Daniel's right. We need to secure this place the best we can. We need a list of any armaments this place has."

"Armaments?" Sister Monroe repeated as if she had never heard the word before. "We don't have any weapons. We're noncombatants."

"Sister, there's no such thing today," Jax corrected, rising to his feet. "Tonight, you fight or you die."

Sister Monroe's jaw dropped open. She tried to say

something, working it up and down, but nothing came out.

"We'll need to get these gates closed and set a watch," I instructed Enoch. I looked at Jax. "They have enough tools in their workshops to make a small armament. Not sure we have the time."

"We have to have the time," Jax pointed out, already heading off to see what he could do.

"This place is crip for being defensible, but we may be able to create a few surprises for them once they enter," Angel said. "I'll need some volunteers."

"Jax will need people to help him with the weapons as well," I said, looking out into the crowd. "Volunteers?"

The prisoners we helped free who were present raised their hands. With both the prisoners we brought and the settlers, we had somewhere close to one hundred and fifty people in the settlement. We'd be lucky if half lived through the night.

A few of the settlers raised their hands, shock still sinking in.

"Enoch, see what you can do," I told him. "I'm going to close the gates."

At the sound of his name, Enoch seemed to snap out of a trance.

He nodded quickly then moved to address his people.

I left him to it.

"These people aren't fighters, Daniel," X cautioned inside my head. "You know what the Voy can do. You only stand toe to toe with them because of your enhancements."

"I know," I said through gritted teeth as I approached the settlement's open gates. "But we can't run. That's what they want. It'll be easier to kill us out in the open at night. The best chance these people have is to stay here and survive until morning."

"How many do you think they'll bring?" X asked, trying to do the math. "A hundred? A thousand?"

"I don't know," I said, moving my mind from the things I didn't have an answer for to those that I did.

The gates were three stories high and made from multiple pieces of white rock all lined together. Each column was just narrower than the width of my shoulders. The rock gates would hold unless the Voy brought in explosives.

I moved over to the right side of the open gate. I put my shoulder into it and began to shove it closed. The gate squeaked and groaned like it had never been closed before.

"The gates have remained open since the settlement was founded," Eli said, jogging up to me. "It's our choice to welcome any traveler that comes our way."

"Yeah, well what does your religion teach about aliens?" I asked.

"Pretty silent about that topic." Eli shrugged. "Here let me help."

Together, we pressed the gate forward. Inch by inch, the old hinges protested, but move they did.

Sister Monroe, then Enoch appeared next to us, aiding in closing the gates. More and more of the settlers joined, pitching in to close the gates for the first time in the history of the settlement.

Other settlers I didn't know started to move the opposite gate shut. Together we forced the large doors closed and secured them in place with a huge metal locking mechanism.

"It's a start," I said.

"I have our people helping Jax and Angel," Enoch reported, composing himself. "We'll make it. The good Lord didn't orchestrate this for us to die tonight. He fights on our side."

"I sure hope so," I said. "We could use all the help we can get. I'm going to check on Jax. See if you can lend Angel a hand."

Enoch nodded and rounded up his people.

I was jogging back toward the workshop when I heard a faint shout. It was the Hessian. I changed course, moving to the rear of the settlement to where the three holes in the ground acted as prison cells.

"Hey, hey, somebody!" the girl yelled. "Hey, what's going on out there?"

"I heard you yelling last night," I said to her, already thinking about what we should do with her. Leaving her in the hole during the attack seemed both right and wrong at the same time. It was probably one of the safest places she could be, but we needed all the help we could get. "The yelling helped, right?"

"Yeah, it was a freaking joy," she sneered. "What were those shots? I heard the sound of a blaster going off."

"Aliens attacking the settlement," I said.

"Yeah, okay." The girl snorted.

I could practically see her eyes roll.

"Seriously, can you get me out of here? I'm clean now, I swear. Last night really set me straight," she begged.

"I'm not sure a single night sees you straight from stim," I answered.

I sensed movement behind me to my left.

Enoch approached with a heavy ring of keys.

"It doesn't seem right to keep her locked in there if

this is going to be our last night—if we are going to fight through the night." Enoch caught himself. "If they were to get to her, she would have no chance."

"Father Enoch?" the girl asked. "Is that you? Come on, you can let me out now. It smells weird in here. I promise I won't try to steal anything else or start any more fires."

I nodded toward Enoch's inquiring eyes.

He knelt down to unlock the bolt holding the circular door closed.

The grate opened on a hinge. Enoch reached in to help out a tall girl who couldn't be out of her late teenage years. She was pretty with long silvery white hair that had to be dyed.

She was skinny, sickly so, the effects of too much stim. Tattoos covered the exposed parts of her arms and came up onto her neck. She had a nose ring and multiple ear piercings. Another ring in her lip and a final one in her eyebrow.

"Thanks, thank you," she said, blinking toward me.

"If you think about running, you should know we weren't kidding about those aliens," I told her. "You wouldn't make it far. Supply ship comes tomorrow morning."

"Seriously, you can drop the whole alien thing," she said as we moved from the rear of the settlement toward the workshop. "I'm not buying it. And I won't run. I can hang out until tomorrow morning and then get a ride back to the city. I—"

As fate would have it, two of the freed prisoners were carrying the corpse of the Voy Angel had shot. Whether they were going to burn it or try and freeze it like the other one I didn't know.

The Hessian stopped in her tracks. She rubbed her eyes like that was going to help.

"Man, I'm tripping so hard," she said. "Maybe I'm not over that stim yet."

"I told you," I said. "Aliens are going to attack the settlement tonight. This is your chance to make up for what you've done and survive in the process."

The girl looked at me and then at Enoch.

"With your penance already paid in the cell and if you agreed to help," Enoch proposed. "We could see about reducing the charges against you. If you promise to stay off the stim, that is."

The Hessian just nodded, trying to figure out what she thought.

"I'll leave you two to figure out the details," I said, moving on toward Jax and the workshop.

Loud ringing and banging came from the building.

I entered to see Jax pounding at steel with the help of a dozen or so freed prisoners and settlers. The place looked more like a forge than a workshop at the moment.

Heat radiated from the benches as tools were used to cut steel and fashion bladed weapons.

Jax caught my eye and motioned me over.

"It's not much, but it'll have to do until we can secure some of the Voy weapons to use against them," Jax said. "We can fashion spears, knives, and swords from the steel-cutting equipment they have, but anything projectile will be tricky. I might be able to get a few crossbows working."

"We'll get weapons for them when it all starts," I agreed with him. "We'll make it work."

"Angel and your abilities will be useful," Jax said with serious thought. "I might have to break out mine tonight. If I do, I'll need you and Angel to talk me down."

The way he said it, the darkness in his voice told me there was so much more to him than met the eye.

I had to ask. "I don't remember what your ability is. How did what Immortal Corp do to us affect you?"

Jax paused. I could see a muscle twitch in his jaw line.

"Let's hope we don't have to be reminded," Jax said. "Come on, you can help us get these spears set up. Angel had a plan to use them in a trap."

EIGHTEEN

THE SPEED at which the recently freed prisoners worked spurred on that of their counterparts inside the settlement. They understood exactly what was on the line, having been prisoners of the Voy--some like Rose, for years.

The settlers latched on to this frantic need to prepare. I wasn't going to tell them everything was going to be okay. Sometimes fear could be a motivator. Right now, it was the driving force behind getting the settlement transitioned into a fortress.

The cold hard truth was that this place was never meant to withstand an attack. With defenses on the walls, it was less a matter of if the Voy were going to break through the walls and more of when.

To combat our weakness, Angel was preparing

traps around the inside of the settlement. With the lack of any explosives, we had to stick to electric wires, flammable liquids, and good old-fashioned spike traps.

The spike traps were set up more to maim than to do any real lasting damage, but if we could hobble the Voy, it would make it easier for any one of us to take them out for good.

The idea was the three of us Pack Protocol members would each watch a wall with the bulk of everyone else protecting the fourth and final wall. We could rotate as needed and provide support where the fighting would be the heaviest.

I found myself at the front gates with Rose, the Hessian girl, and a handful of settlers when the sun lowered behind the dunes.

On the inside of the settlement walls, a catwalk allowed us to see out into the Martian landscape. I held my MK II with my knife and axe in my belt. Rose held on to her blaster. The Hessian girl, along with the others, had spears and a mix of clubs and swords.

I could be sure most of them had never wielded a weapon before in their lives.

Behind us on the ground were a series of spike traps dug by Angel and the Way settlers. We knew exactly where they were. When we'd have to retreat from the wall, we would be safe while the Voy hopefully fell behind us.

"You should really give me that hand cannon of yours." The Hessian girl looked over at me from my left. She eyed my weapon, wiping sweat from her brow despite the lack of heat. "I mean, you're probably better with hand-to-hand fighting anyway, right? What are you, some kind of super-soldier or something?"

"Don't worry about me," I told her, eyeing the droplets of sweat rolling off her brow. "Still coming off the stim? You should get some water in you, maybe some food."

"Threw up all the food." She grimaced as if she could still taste the act. "Got some water in me. Thanks, Dad."

"I'm not old enough to be your dad," I told her, mildly offended.

"Well, stop caring so much," she snapped.

"We're all in this together," Rose said from my right. "Now more than ever, we're all in this together. He's just trying to help."

"Right," the Hessian girl sneered, rolling her eyes. "You're acting like you know anything about me. I see how you eat your food, how you walk. Don't think I don't know you come from money."

"My money or lack thereof means nothing here," Rose said without sounding offended.

"Spoken like someone who has money," the Hessian girl scoffed.

"What's your name?" Rose asked her.

"Oh, now you care?" the girl spat.

"You're always so angry," I told her with a raised eyebrow.

"So deal with it," the girl snarled.

"Oh, I'm not saying that's a bad thing," I said, leaning in toward her. "Anger is great fuel. You'll need it tonight if you're going to live to see the morning. Use that, draw from that when the killing starts."

The girl melted in front of me. She swallowed hard, her dilated eyes, huge.

"Cryx, my name's Cryx," she whispered more than spoke.

"Daniel, eleven o'clock, two hundred meters," X said out loud. "Do you see them?"

I blinked, concentrating on using my night vision courtesy of X. It was just dark enough now to make seeing anything past a few meters sketchy.

"What was that voice, some kind of AI you have?" Cryx asked.

I ignored her. All my attention was where X had instructed. I narrowed my eyes, even craning my neck forward to try and make out anything in the darkness. The night vision made everything look like it had a hue of gold light around it.

Then, past the dunes, I saw them. Voy in six columns marched forward. They didn't seem to be trying to hide their approach in the slightest. They knew exactly how many we were and our lack of weapons.

It seemed the Voy scout Angel caught had only been one of many. They were sure they could beat us, and easily at that. There were no tactics to speak of here, just a straight assault.

"What do you see?" Rose whispered. "How many?"

I couldn't be sure, but if I had to guess, I'd put their number at double, maybe even triple our own.

"Enough to make it a fight," I said out loud. There were others on the wall leaning in to hear my answer. I wasn't going to steal what hope they had left by giving them an honest answer.

This is going to be a long night, I thought, mentally preparing myself for what was going to come. *It's going to be a really long night.*

"I have incoming on the main gate," I said out loud.

Courtesy of X, I had been linked to Angel, Jax, and Enoch via our comm units. Angel and Jax had their own earpieces, and lucky for us, Angel had a spare in case hers died that she had given to Enoch. Enoch watched the rear wall along with the bulk of our forces.

"Let's leave a small defense team at each wall and bring the rest to the front," Angel directed. "Be mindful of the traps just inside the walls."

"On my way," Jax answered.

"How do I talk into this thing?" Enoch asked. "Can you hear me?"

"We can hear you," Angel said, trying to hide her frustration. "You just have to press your finger to your ear and talk."

"Oh, right," Enoch said. "I'm heading over with everyone but five members. If they see anything approach the rear wall, they'll light the alert torch."

Enoch had come up with the idea that each wall should have a powerful spotlight. Since there were only four communication devices amongst us, a wall could use the spotlight to signal they were in trouble. The bright torches would be a beacon to converge upon.

"We'll be outnumbered about two to one," X said inside of my ear. "If they get inside the walls, our chances of survival diminish drastically. You need to get weapons in the hands of the defenders."

"Roger that," I said to X.

The Voy approached so brazenly, so sure of themselves, it made me hate them even more.

They came in their rows of six wide. They wore the armor I had seen them in before. The helmets along with the cloaks and armor-plated chest pieces. They carried swords in sheaths by their side and rifles in the top two of their four hands.

One of the Voy stood apart from the rest with a deep purple cloak and no helmet. He looked up at the wall and shrieked something, yelling in his hard clicks and ticks.

The Voy army lifted their heads into the night and screamed. The sound sent a chill down my spine, not necessarily of fear but of anticipation for what was to come.

The moment was super-charged like a dam ready to burst.

I knew exactly what they were doing. Apparently, it was the same no matter what species you were a part of. Since the beginning of mankind, warriors had used battle cries, posturing, and even armor and helmets to strike fear into their opponents.

I looked up and down the wall. Most of the defenders looked on, wide-eyed. A few were shaking.

To my surprise, Rose seemed like the only one besides me ready for the fight.

The older woman curled her lip.

"I'm not going back. I'm not going back," she repeated under her breath.

"Just in time for the pre-game show," Jax said as he and Angel joined me on the wall.

The Voy were working themselves into a frenzy. Their leader shouted something, then they screamed something back after a brief pause and so on and so on it went.

"We've got to do something," Angel warned, looking from her right to left. "The settlers look like they're going to break at any minute. The freed prisoners aren't far behind."

I wasn't much for motivational speeches. But at that moment, it didn't seem like it was about me; instead, it was time to help the others out. A guy three people down from Rose pissed in his pants. Another was shaking so hard, I thought he was going to hurt himself before the fight even started.

I couldn't blame them. We were facing down aliens. Maybe I was able to move on past that and accept it as our new reality because I had time to soak in the fact. Maybe it had something to do with who I was. I saw a problem and I dealt with it.

Before I could open my mouth and try and provide some kind of rousing speech, Enoch's voice cut through the cold night air.

"Defenders of the Way, hear me now!" Enoch shouted at the top of his lungs. I hadn't given the man enough credit. When he wanted to raise his voice, he could really bring up the volume.

All eyes turned to Enoch, who stood on the wall to my left.

"We may not all believe the same way, but your lack of belief does not sway my own," Enoch began. "We are all here for a reason. Our paths have led us to this point. To be the first bastion of humanity's hope against forces that would snuff out our light. But we are not alone. Warriors have come to stand with us!"

Eyes turned to take in me, Angel, and Jax. Jax even took a bow.

"We will win this night!" Enoch screamed as tears of intensity welled in his eyes. "We must win this fight not for ourselves but to warn those in the cities. We will find a way. We must find a way. Tonight, we do not fight alone. We fight together and the Lord of the Way is with us!"

Settlers and the freed prisoners alike looked at one another, nodding in agreement. I'd say they were far from eager to fight, but at least Enoch's words had kept them from running.

"What do you say we do something crazy and give them heroes to cheer for?" Jax asked with a grim look.

"You sound like you're going to do something stupid," Angel mused, looking over at him.

"You know me," Jax said, glancing down over the wall. He turned his eyes to me. "Danny?"

"They can't kill our spirit," I said, remembering the Pack protocol mantra. "Let's show them what true terror looks like."

NINETEEN

JUMPING over the wall into the open wasn't the smartest idea. I got that. And if I forgot, X was there to remind me.

"Daniel," X said. "I understand the value in being a symbol for these people to rally behind, but putting yourself in the open decreases the likelihood of survival by a significant amount."

"I know," I said, rolling my head around my shoulders while I mentally prepared myself for what I knew needed to be done. "But right now, it's the best hand we have to play."

Jax went first, leaping off the wall to come to a crouched landing position three stories down. Angel went next.

"Our champions!" Enoch shouted to the defenders on the wall. "Will you not rally behind them!?"

A shout from our own side went up to contest the noise the Voy were making with their screeches and clicks.

I planted a foot on the wall and propelled myself forward. I came to a hard landing beside Jax and Angel. The former was taking off his shirt. He had left his weapons behind on the wall.

"We'll bring you back," Angel told him. "It's what needs to be done right now."

Jax clenched his jaw but nodded in agreement.

I still had no idea what I was about to witness, but I understood it was something Jax didn't want to do. He stood rigid, hands clenched at his sides. His focus remained solely on the Voy in front of him.

We were probably within range of each other's weapons, but neither side moved to engage. Not yet. The Voy were still roaring their blood-curdling screams into the night air. Enoch was still leading the cheers from the wall.

"I'm going to go invisible when it starts," Angel told us. "I can do the most damage that way. If we can somehow get the weapons of the fallen Voy to the defenders on the wall—"

"Let us do that," Enoch interjected via the comms.

"I'll coordinate runners to get over the wall, grab the weapons and get back."

We all understood how dangerous that job would be but Enoch was right. The three of us would have our hands full taking on the bulk of the Voy. It was insane. Whatever Jax could do I hoped would even the playing field, but I had my doubts even he would be able to turn the odds in our favor.

The lead Voy in the purple tunic withdrew his sword from its sheath. He clicked something with finality in his voice. As one, the Voy charged our position.

A guttural roar more animal than man came from Jax. I looked over, not believing what I was seeing. Jax's eyes were blood red, not just his pupils, but the entirety of his eyes.

He even looked like he had grown a size or two. His arms were larger, more muscular, and his teeth had fangs.

It was horrible and awe-inspiring at the same moment. Unlucky for me, that moment passed in a blink of an eye. Jax took off, sprinting to meet the enemy, Angel a half step later.

"Get behind Jax!" Angel shouted to me as she ran. "He's our shield in this form."

I ran to obey. If the Voy were taken by surprise at

Jax's change, they didn't falter. A volley of lasers peppered our location as we ran forward. Anyone who has ever shot a weapon while running understands that accuracy becomes a problem. This fact was also true for the Voy.

The rounds that did land spattered across Jax without any real damage done. There was so much I wanted to know about his ability and so many more questions on my mind at the time. I understood this was not the place for either.

The red laser rounds came in closer and more frequently as we closed the gap. Jax outpaced us as his muscular legs ate up the ground between our two forces faster than Angel and I could run.

Angel was right in front of me one minute and gone the next. Activating her camouflage ability was something truly amazing. For the longest time, I thought I was a freak. Five years on the moon with no memory and this insane healing ability and I thought I was the only one.

Now I was running into battle behind an invisible woman and a rage monster. It was the first time I was the most normal one in the bunch.

I heard Jax slam into the front lines of the Voy before I saw it. He hit them dead center like some kind of human battering ram. Screams from the Voy, not in frenzy, but of pain now filled the air.

I could hear bones snap and metal rend as Jax went to work without any other weapons than his bare hands. The animalistic sounds Jax made, the way he tore through them was horrifying. I understood now why he never had wanted to do this, to be this version of himself.

Jax cut through the middle of their lines, leaving the wings of the Voy free to try and engage him or move forward toward the settlement. The Voy moved forward.

I took the left, trusting Angel would take the right.

MK II in hand, I went to work dodging to the side and rolling where I needed to get out of the way of the enemy rounds. That act was pointless. There were simply too many of them and too many weapons aimed at me for me to hope to dodge them all.

I took a round in the right thigh and another in my chest plate. I ran diagonally, trying to give them a hard target while still moving forward. I pumped rounds into their number, aiming for their faces. Even if their helmets could deter a round from my MK II they weren't going to be happy about it.

My point was proven when I double-tapped a pair of

targets. My tungsten steel rounds struck them in the helmets so hard, that even though they didn't penetrate the alien metal at this distance, they did enough to send one to the ground unconscious. The other dropped its weapon, clawing at its helmet as the steel bolt dented the helmet inward into one of its many eyes.

Pain tore at my left shoulder as another round struck me there. Something fell at my feet. I looked down just in time to see a red blinking light cease beeping altogether.

I had just enough time to think, *Son of a—*

The alien explosive detonated, sending me hurtling through the air. I landed in a heap a few meters away from the point of impact. I was still trying to get my bearings. My ears rang, blood pooled into my eyes.

I gasped for breath, trying to figure out where on the battlefield I had been thrown. When I understood where I was, I saw the Voy to my right. Apparently, they had orders to take the settlement first and deal with us only as an obstacle.

While we had taken on the brunt of their attack, the Voy were trickling in toward the wall and the defenders. I was still struggling to my feet when a Voy took notice of me. It stalked toward me, aiming its weapon at my head.

A thin cut opened across its neck a moment later. It

coughed, sputtered, then fell to its knees, trying to stem the flow of blood seeping out of its throat.

Angel appeared from behind the dying Voy.

"Stop messing around," she barked, not offering a helping hand. "Get up."

She was invisible and a second later. No doubt, headed back into the fight.

"Great pep talk," I murmured, pushing myself to my feet.

I scanned the battlefield. Jax was still in the middle of the Voy, throwing haymakers with fists that were as large as my face. A few dozen of the aliens had surrounded him. They cut at him with their blades and hosed him with weapons fire, but to my amazement, Jax was invulnerable to their weapons.

I would have loved to watch the fight unfold. Unfortunately, I had to kill a few dozen Voy before this could all be over.

Despite our best attempts, the three of us, no matter how augmented we were, were not able to stop the Voy from reaching the settlement. We had hindered the bulk of their army, but enemy soldiers were already assaulting the walls.

Worse was that Enoch's plan to have a few runners sprinting around the battlefield grabbing weapons to take back to our own was failing miserably.

The gates had been opened to let a handful of the bravest settlers and freed prisoners out then closed again. I saw Eli, Rose, Cryx, Sister Monroe, and a handful of others sprinting around the battlefield gathering what weapons they could, then heading back to the walls.

The only problem now was that the gates were closed, the scavengers could try and throw the weapons over the wall, but three stories up was going to be difficult, even for Eli, who was physically the strongest among them.

On top of that, the Voy had reached the walls of the settlement. The three-story white stone slabs that would be impossible for humans to scale were only a nuisance for the Voy.

The alien soldiers fired their weapons into the stone wall, making hand and foot holds in the structure.

I rose to my feet, entering the fight again. Despite my recent run-in with the alien explosive, I had managed to hold on to my MK II. I moved to check my charge pack.

"I've been counting," X said in my head. "You have four rounds left. Make them count."

"X," I said with a grim smile. "I've missed you."

Whatever X was about to say next was interrupted by a woman's scream.

I pivoted in time to see a Voy with its sword through Rose's gut. Blood poured out of the older woman's mouth as the alien lifted her off her feet. Cryx cowered behind Rose with an alien rifle in her hands.

I brought my Mk II to bear on the alien, sending a pair of shots that slammed into the back of its skull. It stumbled.

Cryx found the trigger on the alien rifle and let the Voy in front of her have it at point-blank range.

A series of rounds at such close proximity left a gaping hole where the alien's face had once been. The Voy fell to the ground with Rose on top of it.

I sprinted over to Cryx and Rose. Out of the corner of my eye, I saw Sister Monroe and Eli running to the side of the settlement. Eli heaved the weapon up to the wall to waiting defenders.

"We're getting some of the weapons now," Enoch relayed over the comms. "I don't know how much longer we can hold them. They're climbing the wall."

I wish I could have cloned myself in that situation. But I had to deal with what was in front of me at the moment. Rose lay in Cryx's arms, bleeding out.

TWENTY

I SKIDDED to a halt beside them.

"Why—why would you do that?" Cryx asked as hot tears spilled down her cheeks. "You didn't have to do that. You don't even know me."

"But I do," Rose said with a tired smile. Blood leaked down the corners of her mouth. Her eyes began to glaze over. She looked at me and pressed something into my hand. "For you and Cryx. A new start."

She was gone.

"No, wait, no, we have to get her back behind the wall." Cryx was hysterical. "We have bandages and medi—"

"She's gone," I said, rising to my feet. I put the bloody chip Rose had pressed into my hand in my pocket. "Let's go. We can't have you out here anymore. It's not safe. I guess it never was."

Cryx looked numb. I grabbed her by the arm. I pushed her toward where Sister Monroe fed Eli weapons. He heaved them up over the wall to the waiting hands of the defenders.

The two of them were the last ones alive of those who had tried to run out and gather weapons to give our side a chance.

Cryx and I ran over to them, picking up what fallen weapons we could along the way. By the time we got there, I had three more rifles and Cryx carried four in her arms.

"It's not enough," Sister Monroe said as Eli and I hurled the weapons over the wall. "We need more. We have to go out and get more."

"She's right. With these, that makes only thirteen we were able to get," Eli said. "We need to go out again and get more of them."

"No time," I told them. "You three need to get back inside the wall."

"How?" Cryx asked.

She had a point. We were on the left side of the settlement just around the corner of the main wall where the Voy assaulted the gates. A quick look told me the walls defended by Enoch and the bulk of the settlers and freed prisoners was in the process of being overrun.

We wouldn't be getting through that way.

Jax was still raging around the field of battle, tearing any Voy dumb enough to get close to him in half.

Angel was nowhere to be seen.

"What's going on?" Angel said, appearing right beside me.

"Holy crip!" Sister Monroe blurted, covering her mouth as soon as the curse word flew out.

I had to admit I almost peed myself too. Angel was as quiet as the trained assassin she was created to be.

"The walls are falling," I told her. "We need to get inside."

"Stand back," Angel said, taking out her silenced blaster. She strategically placed a group of foot and handholds into the rock fence in front of us just like the Voy had at the front.

I should have thought about that myself. Not that the last two rounds in my MK II would have gotten us far up the wall.

"Come on, let's go." Angel prodded them forward. "We're out of time."

Cryx went first followed by Sister Monroe and Eli. I looked back to where Jax roared into the night. He must have gotten farther and farther away. Even with my night vision, I couldn't see him. He was lost behind a dune or around the opposite side of the settlement.

"Jax?" I asked.

Angel shook her head, a haunted glimmer in her eye.

"He's no good to us right now," Angel said, climbing the wall. "He's lost to the blood rage."

I understood there was a lot I wasn't getting at the moment. But all my questions would have to wait. Screaming was heard from the wall above. The Voy had ascended the front gates despite the best laid plans of the defenders.

"Your best bet now is to get them behind the traps and make use of the weapons you gathered from the Voy," X said inside my head. "Tell them to retreat inside the settlement and let the Voy fall on the traps."

I grunted an understanding as I pulled myself over the ledge. It wasn't like I had to sound the retreat. The defenders who remained on their feet were fleeing the wall in terror.

The Voy had ascended and were making quick work of any of those too slow in their retreat.

"We can't—we can't hold them," Enoch gasped.

I could hear the pain in his voice. It was clear he was injured to some degree.

"Get back, behind the traps," Angel shouted. "Retreat!"

The yells filled the night air as the Voy clicked and screeched their cries of premature victory. The catwalk inside the wall was slick with blood. The fluid belonged to a few Voy but mostly the defenders on the wall.

Bodies littered the ground on both sides of the wall.

I jumped down off the catwalk onto the inside of the settlement. A short sprint brought me to where Angel had taken command of setting up a rough barricade. A long waist-high wall of white rock had been dragged in to use as cover.

The idea was that we would remain in plain sight and let the Voy charge us, falling into the traps while we laid into them with their own weapons.

Right now, the Voy were opening the gates for the rest of their number to gain entrance into the settlement.

"We need everyone watching the other walls here now," Angel yelled at three settlers who looked on wide-eyed at the approaching Voy. "Look at me and focus!"

Angel screamed these words, slapping one of the men who seemed lost somewhere between shock and confusion.

"Go, get them here now and tell each wall to bring their fuel with them," Angel instructed.

I saw Enoch sitting behind the defensive barrier that was erected. He held a right hand to his stomach where a Voy round had caught him. A woman I didn't know tended to him.

"Everyone with a weapon, I need you ready to fire!" Angel shouted to the few defenders who remained. There had to be forty still on their feet with no more than thirteen Voy rifles between them.

"I'll hold here," I told Angel, catching on to her plan. "When the fuel comes, you'll be the best suited to disperse it amongst them."

"Roger that," Angel said to me, extending a fist. "Hold the line. Buy me ten minutes."

"Ten minutes is an eternity," I remarked, only half teasing.

"You can do it," Angel said, going invisible once more. "We're the best."

A few of the Voy were trading pot shots with our

impromptu barricade. They were doing it more to keep our heads down than actually wanting to hit us. Their strategy was becoming clear. They'd use longer distance weapons fire in an attempt to keep our heads down while they rushed in close, giving them a chance to use their blades as well as their blasters.

"Heads low!" I yelled down the line. "Hold your fire! Not yet!"

The scared faces looked back at me, complying with my order. They still looked terrified. They were holding on, but only on by their fingertips.

I took a peek over the edge of the barricade. The gates were wide open now. The Voy were forming ranks again. Unbeknownst to them, right in front of the traps Angel had lain. We just had to hold them for a few minutes.

When the Voy charged this time, there was no excited war chant, no clicks and screeches in unison. The same leader in the purple robe led them. His own blood caked the left side of his face.

They had misjudged us so far. This was not the easy victory they had assumed before. They were ready this time, prepared for a battle. Lucky for us, we had the traps waiting for them.

With a single click of his throat, the enemy

commander sent the order down the line of Voy to charge. The Voy that did remain were a fraction of what they had once been before. There couldn't be more than sixty of them now, still in fighting condition.

"We can do this," X said out loud for all to hear. "We can beat them!"

The Voy came at a run, pounding over the sandy ground. One second they charged us in a line of armored bodies, the next they fell victim to the many traps set by Angel and those working with her.

Screams ripped from their throats as they fell to the carefully laid foot snares. Each pit was only a meter wide by a meter length and a meter deep. Angel placed the metal knife-like spike pointing up then covered them with a cloth and a layer of sand.

The trap was primitive at best, but it was effective and there were hundreds of them. We had known where each one was placed and skirted the area when we pulled back.

The Voy fell on them with agony. In their haste to attack, the first line went down screaming in anguish while the second and third line fell on top of them.

A mass of angry and pained Voy throats lifted to the dark sky. In the shadows the moons and stars provided, I gave the command.

"Fire everything you've got and don't stop firing until your weapons are dry!" I shouted. "Everything you've got, let them have it!"

The defenders didn't disappoint. Thirteen rifles poured into the mass of Voy along with rocks, spears, and even the few crossbows Jax had managed to build out of the steel.

I pulled my MK II out, choosing my targets. I only had two rounds left. I needed to be smart. As fate would have it, the perfect target appeared on the battlefield. The purple-robed leader emerged at the forefront of the screaming pack of Voy, who pushed over one another, only to fall into another round of traps.

The Voy leader was smart as he walked forward, only stepping where one of his soldiers had already tested the ground.

He screamed at his soldiers, urging them forward. He carried a sword in one of his upper right hands, and a rifle in the lower two arms.

He looked at me, pointing his sword at our lines.

"Daniel, the leader may be—"

"Got him," I said to X, firing my last rounds at the Voy commander.

It was a perfect shot. Just as the Voy leader opened his mouth to scream at his men to move forward, my rounds hit him in the face and open mouth.

A splattering of blood and brain matter flew behind him as he fell to the ground, lifeless.

Against all odds, we were managing to hold them. Now, without a leader, it was up to each enemy soldier to find it within themselves to move forward. The traps were enough to hobble them, injure them, and even hold them for a moment, but they wouldn't kill them.

The firepower from our lines would have to do that and the defenders we had firing the weapons weren't exactly crack shots. The red laser rounds were going wide to the left, to the right, and above. I guessed that only one in every four actually found a mark.

"Incoming," Angel said via the comms. "Are they trying not to hit them on purpose?"

"Right?" I said, going over to a shaking settler who held a rifle in his hands. I beckoned to him. He knew exactly what I was asking for, handing me the rifle like he had never wanted it in the first place.

I rested the butt of the weapon to my shoulder, aiming slightly down the barrel.

"Where are you?" I asked, finding target after target to put down. The enemy was nearly out of the minefield of traps. It would be over if they got to our lines. There was nowhere else to fall back to.

"I'm in their lines," Angel whispered in a hurry.

I picked off Voy after Voy who got close enough to make a rush for our lines. Enemy fire hit me in the gut and shoulder, sending ripples of torment through my body. I ignored it all. What happened now meant the survival or death of this settlement.

The smell of fuel permeated the air. Angel's plan to run within their line and splash the fluid around was working. I wasn't the only one that caught the smell.

Voy who fought their way through the traps and incoming weapon fire paused now to smell the air.

To the right of the Voy, I saw a flare tossed into the center of the mix. The bulk of the Voy forces went up in an inferno. Red-hot flames licked the cold night air as Voy screeched and clicked in misery.

Those who were able to get out of the flames were met with my rounds as well as that of the remaining defenders.

We killed them with impunity.

It's either them or us, I justified in my head as I focused on the Voy who stumbled out of the flames toward our lines. *It's them or us.*

Angel popped to life beside me.

"Holy crip!" I yelled, almost turning my weapon on her. "You really have to give some kind of war—"

"Daniel," X warned.

The words died on my lips. Angel was a mess of blood and open wounds. Running through the Voy lines, she had been shot by our side's own sporadic fire multiple times.

Angel fell to her knees beside me.

TWENTY-ONE

"ANGEL, HEY, HEY," I said, dropping to my knees. "Stay with me. Hang in there."

She was flushed. If her wounds were healing, I couldn't tell.

"I'll be fine," Angel said with a weak grin. "I just don't heal as quickly as you do. I need to rest. You'll have to get Jax."

Angel slumped forward.

I moved just in time to catch her. I lifted her in my arms and took her back to where the defenders stood behind the waist-high wall.

"She's just unconscious," X told me. "She needs to rest and let her body do what it wants to do. We can help her by stopping the bleeding, but she'll be fine, Daniel. She's going to make it."

"I need help," I called out. "We need some bandages."

Sister Monroe and Cryx were by my side a moment later, taking Angel from me.

"Did we do it?' Cryx asked with wide bloodshot eyes. "Did we really just stop an alien invasion?"

"The Invasion's still coming," I told her. "But we stopped this attack."

Cryx nodded. She moved off with Sister Monroe to take care of Angel.

I stood there surveying the landscape with the rest of the defenders who remained. Our numbers had been easily cut in half, maybe even more. The smell of burnt meat that I knew was Voy filled the air around us.

Eli came over to me. The large man held tears in his eyes. I got it. We were all a bit numb at the moment from fatigue. For most, this was their first time taking a life.

"How—how do you do it?" Eli asked, not looking at me but instead the still burning Voy bodies. "How do you forget about all of this and act like a normal person ever again?"

"I'm not sure forgetting this is in the cards, no matter how much we might want to," I told him. "You learn to accept it and deal with it. It's a part of you for the rest of your life."

An animalistic bellow reminded me what Angel said. I needed to go and find Jax. I didn't have the first clue on how to talk him down from whatever animalistic urge had possessed him. I had no idea what the scientists did to him while turning him into a member of the Pack Protocol, but I couldn't leave him like that.

The madness I saw in his eyes when he made the transition was one of pure fury.

"You get the wounded taken care of and close the gates," I instructed Eli as I trotted toward the entrance of the settlement.

"Where are you going?" Eli asked, half-panicked.

"I'm going to go meet a monster," I called over my shoulder.

I made my way past the smoking Voy corpses out through the front of the gates and into the desert beyond.

Jax's roars came again, this time closer.

It was a strange thing for me to feel nervous. Very few things in this world put me on edge anymore. After all, I had come face to face with murderous aliens and killed them.

Trotting into the dark desert of Mars to find a man gone animal was still enough to get me worried.

"Remember to approach slowly and talk him down," X advised. "We don't know how much of Jax is actually in there at this point. Weapons had no effect on him. The Voy blasters and blades didn't puncture his skin."

"Right," I said.

I found Jax staring up at the night sky, breathing heavy. He looked like he had grown a size or two in his current condition. The guy was already larger than I was, but now he was near seven feet tall with a back that rippled with muscle.

His chest rose up and down as he panted. He turned when he heard me approach. Those blood red eyes took me in with a gleam of rage.

"Easy," I told him, opening both hands to show I had no weapons. "It's me, Daniel."

Jax just stared.

I walked around him to get a better view.

X was right. There were no visible wounds on him. He was covered in dark Voy blood.

"Can you hear me in there?" I asked. "Jax, it's me. Can you understand me?"

Jax's chest fell up and down as he eyed me. He opened his mouth like he was going to say something. Fangs showed past his teeth. No words came out.

"We need to get you back to the settlement in—in

a more normalish form," I told him. "Can you turn back?"

Jax failed to hear the figure behind him. A wounded Voy was rising to his feet on the dune. It lifted a blaster from its side.

Instinct kicked in. In a single fluid movement, I withdrew the knife at my belt and hurled it through the dark air at the Voy. The blade sank deep into the soft part of its throat between its helmet and chest piece.

The Voy fell backward soundlessly behind the dune.

Jax turned back into the rage monster he had been before. He opened his mouth wide, showing me impossibly large canines. His muscles bulged.

"No," I said, opening both hands again and pointing them forward to face him, "There was a Voy on the hill. I just killed him. I wasn't throwing the knife at you."

Jax took a quick look behind him. Since the Voy had fallen back behind the dune, there was no evidence of the body.

"Great," I said out loud as Jax lunged for me.

I ducked a meaty fist then rolled out of the way as he tried to grab me with his free hand.

"Jax, stop, that's enough!" I tried not to sound like

I was talking to some kind of misbehaving dog. "Jax, it's me."

It seemed Jax was past all rational thought at the moment.

He leapt at me, trying to tackle me to the ground.

Whatever happened, I knew if he got a hold of me, it was all over. And in his current state, I was not sure if he would stop at taking me out of the fight.

I dove to the side out of his leap. He roared at me, connecting with a right fist that felt like a truck hit me. Stars exploded across my vision as my pain receptors registered the blow. I staggered to the side just in time to step in close and slam my fist into his face.

Hitting him felt like connecting with a brick wall. I landed three blows with Jax just looking at me before I figured I should probably abandon this means of attack. If the Voy weapons couldn't get to him then my fists had little chance.

"Okay, hey," I said, dropping my hands. "Maybe hitting you isn't the best way to get through to you."

Jax grinned. Without any effort, he picked me up and hurled me through the night air. I slammed hard into a sand dune ten meters away.

The wind knocked out of me, I struggled to my hands and knees.

"I don't think this is working," X said out loud.

"Really? What would give you that idea?" I asked.

Before I could regain my feet or X could respond, Jax was standing over me again. He lifted me for a second time and hurled me through the brisk night once more.

I crashed in a heap onto the sandy floor of the Martian landscape.

"I'm open to suggestions," I groaned as I fought my way to my feet.

"I don't think he wants to kill you," X surmised. "He's had opportunities in the last two attacks and instead opted to throw you instead of snap your bones."

"Great, so he's just going to play with me like a dog with a bone for a while," I said, tracking Jax's movements as he approached again. "Any ideas?"

"If you can get me close enough for a short period of time, I may be able to help," X answered. "There is a chance that, like an animal, that a high-regulated frequency may act to—"

"English, X," I said, trying to hide the frustration in my voice.

"Get me close and I'll set off a sound that should calm him," X answered.

That was all there was time for. Jax was on top of me again.

This time, there was a grin on his face.

Well, at least he's not trying to turn me into a corpse, I thought. *That's something.*

When Jax reached for me with both arms, I batted his hands away and jerked to my left, his right. In a practiced move I'd used before in the bars of the moon, I maneuvered myself around his back. I had to jump to get him in a headlock. My legs wrapped around his midsection.

My arms around his neck felt like I was trying to choke out a piece of metal. Jax roared with a gurgle as I pressed down. He tried shaking me off then reaching behind him to grab hold of me. His arms were too muscular to give him that range of motion.

"Anytime now," I grunted.

"It's already started," X said. "You won't be able to hear it."

Sure enough, Jax's frantic movements began to slow. Instead of his manic attempts to throw me off, he grunted something. His hands fell to his sides.

"There we are," I said. "Jax, I'm going to let you go now. Can I let you go now?"

I felt his head nod in the affirmative.

I released my hold and gently slipped off his back.

Whatever signal X had found was working.

"X, remind me to give you a raise," I said.

"Noted," X answered.

Jax fell to his knees, docile.

"Jax, we need you back, buddy," I said, looking him in the eye. "Angel's hurt. She's going to pull through fine, but I bet knowing that you're safe and by her side will make her feel better."

That focused Jax's attention on me. Angel's name seemed to have a serious effect on him.

In front of me, his red eyes transitioned back to normal. He shrank with some of the muscle receding into his body. The fangs in his mouth turned back into normal teeth.

A few seconds later, the version of Jax I knew knelt in front of me on the sandy ground.

"I—I'm sorry," Jax said. He sounded exhausted. "Did I hurt you?"

"I'm fine," I told him. "You forgot who you're talking to. Can you walk?"

"Yeah, yeah, it just takes me a minute to come down," Jax said. "Angelica?"

"She's safe and resting," I answered. "Come on. Let's get out of here."

TWENTY-TWO

WHAT THE SETTLERS lacked in fighting ability, they made up in sheer work ethic. There wasn't a lazy individual amongst the settlers or the freed prisoners and if there had been, they were dead now.

About sixty defenders had made it through the night. Those left in the wake of the first real battle between humans and aliens were bone weary. Still, they managed to secure the gates and pile the dead Voy bodies outside, while laying the human fallen inside the settlement walls.

The sun was just beginning to rise. Jax was with a sleeping Angel and I had found my bunk, giving in to much needed rest. I was dead on my feet. Sure, my body healed a hundred times faster than anyone else's, but it had to pull that energy from somewhere. I hit the pillow dreaming about food.

"Daniel, Daniel," X's voice woke me. "Daniel, wake up."

"Just two more minutes," I mumbled.

"Daniel, you've been asleep for six hours. The supply ship is arriving," X said.

That got my attention.

"Six hours," I said, sitting up in my bunk and blinking hard. My stomach felt like an empty cave of nothing. It growled something fierce. "I feel like I just shut my eyes."

"I was going to let you sleep, but I thought you should know," X answered.

"You did good." I yawned and stretched.

My eyes drifted across the empty room Angel, Rose, Jax, and I shared before the attack.

Memories of Rose, the woman who would have made a wonderful member of the Pack Protocol, played through my mind. She had never given up and the same warrior spirit that lived in me I was sure resided in her as well.

My hand instinctively went to my pocket, where I placed the chip she had pressed into my hand. I sighed, relieved that the chip was still present.

I hopped off the bed and walked to the door.

Opening the door to the small building nearly blinded me. The sun shone down in all of its midday glory.

I blinked, trying to give my eyes time to adjust.

Shouts were coming from the defenders who were awake. They were moving to open the main gates that had been shut after Jax and I entered the settlement walls.

I jogged over, feeling weak. Cryx was there eating some kind of protein pouch. She looked like she had gotten some sleep herself.

"Supply ship came in," Cryx said with a gentle shake of her head. "Can't wait to see the look on their faces when they see the aliens."

"Hey, where'd you get that?" I asked, eyeing her pouch hungrily.

"From that building with the food they have over there. I have an extra one if you—"

As soon as Cryx lifted the extra protein pack out of her pocket, I grabbed it as if it were life itself and started to power it down.

"My gosh, remember to breathe," Cryx said as I chugged the contents of the pouch.

The protein pouch was chocolate-flavored and tasted like the best thing I had ever put into my mouth. That was one good thing about being so hungry. Everything tasted wonderful.

With my stomach happy with me for the time being, I directed my attention to the open gates. I was surprised to see Enoch up. He walked with a cane and slightly hunched. I could imagine there were a series of bandages under his clothing.

Still, the settlement leader was on his feet and ready to lead his people.

The supply ship was a short bulky thing made for short distance travel. A clear window in the front let us see the pilot and copilot of the ship. They had touched down somewhere outside of the settlement walls and coasted on fat tires to the gates.

It was clear by their expression they had already seen the alien corpses. Both pilot and copilot looked pale with mouths wide open. The pilot, a balding man with a slight gut, spoke via the external ship speakers.

"Enoch what's going on here? What—what are these things?" he asked.

"Justin, it's good to see you," Enoch shouted. He looked like he might fall. Sister Monroe appeared at his side to support him. "By the Lord's will are we glad to see you. We'll tell you everything, but please, we need access to your radio. There's a lot going on here that is far beyond us, my friend."

The pilot looked at his copilot, a woman somewhere in her fifties. She just nodded.

The supply ship coasted into the settlement. Its thruster died with a whine as the pilot and copilot exited.

I left the bureaucracy to Enoch. I had neither the patience nor the time to explain to someone else that aliens were real.

Angel hobbled out of a building to my left with Jax's support, looking like she had seen better days. Her right arm was in a sling. She was a touch paler with a grim look on her face.

She jerked her head toward me, then the supply ship.

I followed her and Jax into the ship under the protests of the pilot.

"Hey, hey, you can't just go in there," he yelled at us. He looked like he might actually move to try and stop us.

"Trust me, you don't want to do that right now." I looked at him with a hard stare. "We've had a rough night."

Justin withered under my stare. Enoch touched his arm and went back to explaining what had happened.

I ducked into the wide interior of the supply ship. Unlike dropships, this craft was much smaller. There were the pilot and copilot's seats and a side open area in the rear for supplies. That was pretty much the extent of the ship. Right now, it was loaded down with boxes and crates of food stuffs, medical supplies, and construction materials.

Jax helped Angel to the front of the ship, where she sat heavily in the pilot's seat. Jax took the copilot's seat and I stood behind them.

Angel was hiding her pain level well, but I knew she was hurting.

"Stop looking at me like I'm going to die." Angel glared at me then melted into a smile "We don't all heal as quickly as you."

"I mean, unless you can't be injured at all," I said, looking at Jax.

"It comes at a price, a heavy price," Jax said, clenching his jaw. "When I let go and turn into that thing—I lose it. I could have hurt someone on our side. The messed up part is that I like it. There's nothing like that feeling of letting go and surrendering to my most animalistic nature."

"You wouldn't hurt any of us," Angel assured him, placing her hand on Jax's. "You're getting better."

"No, it's getting harder to come back from it." Jax gritted his teeth. "I'm afraid one day I won't be able to come back at all."

"We won't let that happen," Angel said, giving his

hand a squeeze. "You shouldn't have to change anytime soon. The cavalry is on the way."

Angel picked up the radio and punched in a series of numbers to a specific channel. She allowed the radio to play through the ship's speakers so we could all hear.

"Hello, Comstock's Antiquities, how may I help you?" an elderly man's voice came over the line.

I was sure Angel had pressed a wrong number, when to my surprise, she answered.

"It looks like a storm's coming," Angel said as if it were a memorized phrase. "The way will be dangerous."

"Even in the most brutal of storms there is an end," the man responded. "And those capable of weathering the very worst. Hold, please."

The line went silent.

"Angelica, Jax, is that you?" Wesley Cage's voice asked. "What happened? I was about to bring a team myself to come and get you after you missed your last check in."

"I have you on speaker with Jax and Daniel," Angel answered. "Preacher sacrificed himself to get us out. We were right about everything, Cage. The aliens are here and they're building an army. They've already attacked a Way settlement. We held them back, but they'll come again with more weapons and soldiers."

"We need to get you back home," Cage said through a tense voice. "I'm glad you're all safe."

"We have to go back for Preacher," I said, not necessarily knowing how I felt about talking to Wesley Cage again. The last time I saw him back on Earth, I was assaulting his forces and taking one of the Immortal Corp dropships with a horde of Reapers at my back.

"Preacher knew what he was doing," Cage said. "He bought us this chance to get organized before they come. We have to prepare. We'll go back for him, but not now."

My heart tore inside my chest. I could only guess what they were doing to him back at that base. Still, there was truth to what Cage said. If we went now, we might be able to get him. If we went with an army behind us, we had a much better chance of succeeding.

"Angel, I need you to come back," Cage continued. "We need to debrief and regroup. I can have a team there to pick you up in a few hours. Stay put at the Way settlement. I'm looking at the map now. There's only one out in that direction."

"We'll be here," Angel answered. "Hurry."

"I'm coming personally," Cage answered. "I'm on my way now."

The line went dead.

We stood there for a minute in silence.

I could only guess at what was going through Angel's and Jax's minds, but I knew what I was thinking about. I was about to head back to the company that I swore to take down. I was going into the den of the very murderers who had taken out Amber. The ones who created me.

I wasn't sure how to feel.

"Are we going to do this?" Jax asked. "Are we going to leave Preacher behind?"

Angel tapped the dashboard in front of her.

"We debrief and regroup," Angel said, thinking out loud. "Two more days max. Then we go back for him. He bought us time to warn everyone else. We owe it to him to use it."

"And if Immortal Corp won't let us go back in two days?" I asked.

"Then they can go float themselves," Angel said. "I'll go back even without their permission."

"I'm in," Jax confirmed. "I'm not going to leave him to die there."

"Two days," I agreed. "Two days to warn humanity of the alien threat before we go in again."

Angel and Jax made a move to leave the supply ship. When I stayed behind, Jax arched his brow.

"I have a contact at the Galactic Government I need to warn," I said, looking at the radio.

Jax and Angel traded glances.

"We need all the help we can get," I pointed out.

"Go ahead, I can't argue with you there," Jax answered. He left the ship, leaving Angel in his wake.

"We should see how Immortal Corp wants to deal with this before we go off making our own plans," Angel warned. "We're in over our heads here, Daniel."

"Yeah, I'm not a fan of putting my fate in Immortal Corp's hands for multiple reasons," I told her.

"Fair enough," Angel acknowledged, leaving the ship.

"X, you still have the code that Captain Valentine left us?" I asked.

"I don't forget a thing," X said, reading off the channel to me.

It was a long shot. I had only met the woman once. But we had fought and bled together. That counted for something. I also knew she had a daughter on Mars. I'd be able to use that to strike a chord and get her to help. At least I hoped so. The fate of the galaxy as we knew it could very well depend on this call.

TWENTY-THREE

"HELLO?" Captain Zoe Valentine answered the call in not an unfriendly way.

"Hello, Captain Valentine?" I asked.

"Yes, who is this?" she asked.

"My name is Daniel Hunt," I answered, trying not to start the conversation off awkward. "You and I recaptured Aleron Jacobs when he tried to break free from Galactic Government custody on the moon. We took the dropship together to Earth."

"Oh yes." The captain's voice took a step toward friendly but wasn't quite there yet. "Daniel, how can I help you?"

Oh, boy, I thought to myself. *This is going to be the hard part. How do you tell her? Maybe I should have thought this through some more.*

"Daniel, are you there?" Captain Valentine asked.

"I'm here," I answered, clearing my throat. "I'm calling you because you're the only person I know in the Galactic Government. I need to warn you and the GG of a threat here on Mars."

The other end of the line was quiet for a moment. I guessed there were going to be a lot of pauses in this conversation as the captain decided what to do with the information I was sending her.

"I'm not sure I'm the right person to report in to," Captain Valentine responded. "I'm stationed here on Earth at the Hole in New Vegas shuttling prisoners to and from the moon. You know this."

"I do," I said, choosing my words carefully. I needed her on my side, not to piss her off. "But you're the only one I can trust in the Galactic Government right now. There's something happening on Mars that goes far beyond either one of us."

Pause again.

"I have a feeling I'm going to regret asking you, but what's going on over there?" Captain Valentine asked. "Are you in some kind of trouble?"

"Not just me, all of us," I answered. "There's an enemy threat here. An enemy on a very large scale that plans to attack Mars and then move to the moon and finally Earth."

"Who, how did you come across this information?"

"I've seen them myself. I know it's a lot to believe, but you have to, so much depends on it."

"Who is it? Who's behind this threat that you're speaking of? Phoenix? One of the private companies?"

This is it, I thought to myself. *This is where we have a chance or she hangs up on me and thinks I'm one sandwich short of a picnic.*

"Zoe," I said, using her first name. "This is going to be hard to believe. There are—foreign invaders on Mars. They're building a forward base as we speak. They've already attacked one of the outlying settlements here."

"Foreign invaders?" Captain Valentine repeated the words. "Daniel are you trying to tell me there are aliens on Mars?"

"I know how it sounds, and trust me, I wish this were some kind of joke, but I have proof," I said, trying to anticipate what she might say next. "I can show you. We have bodies."

"I—I'm not really sure what's going on with you," the captain continued. I could practically see her raised eyebrow on the other side of the line. "You seemed like a good guy. That's why I gave you this channel, but if you're—"

"X, can you transmit images to her?" I asked quietly as the captain went on.

"Yes, I store images that I think may be of use," X answered. "I'll send some I have now."

"—If this is what you're going to use this channel for, please don't call again," Zoe said. "I'm busy enough trying to take care of a company of praetorians. I don't need…"

Her voice trailed off.

There was no need to ask if she had received the images.

"These are the ones I sent," X said inside my head.

In my field of view, a small window popped up in the lower right hand corner of my eyesight. X cycled slowly through images she had taken of the Voy and their facilities. I would be lost without her. She had the common sense to take multiple photos of the alien base as well as their weapons.

"How—how did you do this?" Zoe asked. "Some kind of photo manipulation? This isn't funny."

"I'm not trying to be funny," I said softly. I sensed an opening. Zoe's voice had shifted from annoyed to worried. I wasn't sure if she was going to believe me yet, but she was on the way. "I know how crazy all of this sounds. But they're real. They're growing in numbers before they attack, but they'll attack soon.

Please, Zoe, at least check it out. Not for me, but for all the lives that would be lost if you believe there is even a one percent chance this can be true."

I hadn't wanted to bring her daughter into this. That was a low blow I'd use only if I absolutely had to. Zoe was smart. She would put two and two together.

"Daniel, they'll pass this off as some kind of joke, even if I do want to believe you," Zoe answered. "Aliens aren't real."

"You have to, Zoe," I answered. "I hate to put this on you, but it's on you now. You have to get someone to come check. I can send you the coordinates. You have to convince someone in the GG that this is worth looking into. I have alien bodies with me as proof. Once they see one of them in real life, there won't be any doubt in their minds. If you can't get them to come out here, at least let me work out a way to get a body to you."

"There's a major that owes me a favor—Daniel, if this is some kind of joke, I want you to know that I am personally going to find you and see you take your last breath," Zoe threatened, letting the wave of pent-up anger boil over. "I mean it."

"I know you do," I said. "No joke, this is serious."

"Is this your private channel?" Zoe asked.

"Yes."

"Let me see if I can call in a favor and we can get you to bring in the evidence you have," Zoe said with a long sigh. "I can't believe we're talking about aliens here, but those images are beyond disturbing. If I can get him to agree to a meeting, you'll have to bring the body. No one else, you."

"Okay," I agreed.

I hadn't forgotten about Immortal Corp coming or going back to free Preacher, but I could hear how strained Zoe was on the other line. She was one wrong answer away from backing out of all of this. I didn't blame her.

"Thank you," I told her.

"Don't thank me yet. I haven't done anything," Zoe said. "You know, if these images are fake, we're both going to get into a lot of trouble."

"If even a fraction of you thinks they could be real, then that's all the reason you need to take a chance," I answered. "For all the many valid reasons you have to hang up on me, you haven't. They're here, Zoe. I don't have all the answers myself. But I know the threat is at our doorstep. I know if we don't do something soon, it'll be too late."

Another long pause.

"Stay close to your comm channel," Zoe said. "I'll be in touch."

The line went dead.

I let out a long pent-up sigh I didn't know I was holding in. I sank deeper into the captain's seat.

"Are you okay?" X asked. "I mean, that seems like a silly question now that I say it out loud."

"I know what you meant," I answered. "I guess I have to be. I did all I could do. It's up to the captain now. And we have one more call to make."

"Samantha?" X asked. "Or the other one?"

"I'm not sure how much good Sam could do right now," I said. "She and her family have been through a lot already. We need to contact the other one. If her organization rivals Immortal Corp for resources, they have to have a clue what's going on here."

"And let's not forget about Phoenix," X said. "We saw the mechs they have in the Vault on Earth. They could be of use as well."

"Agreed, but one at a time." I massaged my temples. "I miss the days of throwing drunks out of bars on the moon. Never thought I'd be saying that."

"You're changing now, for the better," X said. "I'm not sure if you realize that yet, but it's true. You're losing that hard edge, some of the calluses of the past. Your scars will never go away, but at least your wounds are closed."

"You're making too much sense, X," I said, shaking

my head free of emotional thoughts. I needed to be focused for this next call. "You have the channel she gave us?"

"Have it saved," X answered. "Here we go."

Unlike the captain's call where she answered, this one beeped a few times, then a mechanical voice answered.

"User is unavailable," the robotic voice informed us. "If you wish to leave a message, you may do so at this time."

A long beep followed.

"I'm not sure if you gave me a bogus channel or this is just how you do things at The Order," I said, pausing to gather my thoughts. I had been prepared to talk to the masked stranger again, not leave a message.

I shifted uncomfortably in my seat, craning my neck to look behind me into the ship. With as much animosity as Immortal Corp and the Order had for one another, I wasn't sure Jax and Angel would take kindly to me making the call.

"There's something going on, on the uninitiated side of Mars you should know about," I said. "I'm going to send you pictures and coordinates. It doesn't matter what happened in the past. Whose faction wronged someone else's first or any of that. What matters is our survival. I've seen them. The only way we beat them is together."

I ended the transmission feeling one of the many weights I carried lift off my shoulders.

"Well, at least that's done," I said out loud. "Now for our reunion with Immortal Corp."

"What are you going to do if you see the three founders again?" X asked.

I knew exactly who X was talking about. The three figures wrapped in shadow who had given Amber's kill order. One woman missing a finger. The man with the deep voice and the other man who sat silent.

"I'm going to kill them," I answered, rising from my seat. "If I have the opportunity, I'm going to make them pay."

TWENTY-FOUR

TRUE TO HIS WORD, Wesley Cage arrived in an all-black Immortal Corp dropship before dinner.

By that time, we had the Voy bodies quarantined to a section of the settlement. Those Voy who made it into the walls were mostly burned, but the ones who died outside the walls were still usable specimens. I imagined Immortal Corp would be eager to get their hands on them.

After the events of the night, those who survived opted to take our advice and head back to the city. The supply ship was emptied and followers of the Way as well as the freed prisoners piled in.

Angel and Jax went to greet Wesley Cage while I said my goodbyes to Enoch, Sister Monroe, Eli, and Cryx.

"You were sent to us when we needed you the most," Sister Monroe said, catching me off guard in a hug.

I couldn't remember how long it had been since I hugged someone back. I tried not to make the act awkward now, but it was an act in futility.

I wrapped my arms around her and patted her on the back before letting go.

"Well, it was kill or be killed," I said, trying to brush off her praise.

"It was more than that." Sister Monroe planted a kiss on my cheek. "If you ever want a different path, the Way is waiting for you."

Lucky for me, Eli saved me from having to give an answer.

"You were the right man for the job," Eli said, pumping my hand. "Thank you."

Eli stepped back and Enoch limped over to me. He was hunched with the cane in his right hand. His face looked a shade paler, but his smile never wavered.

"Whatever you do or do not believe, I know you were sent to us when we needed you the most." Enoch looked over his shoulder to where Angel and Jax stood on the opposite side of the settlement. "You all were."

"Don't want to burst your bubble," I said. "But

maybe it wasn't meant to be at all. Maybe you being out here just cost a lot of people their lives."

"Maybe we were always meant to be here to provide shelter for you and the freed prisoners," Enoch answered. "To not have your voice, but all of our voices traveling back to the cities to raise awareness. To have multiple alien bodies as proof of what happened here."

"How can you take so much on faith?" I asked.

"If we lose faith and hope, we have nothing," Enoch said. His eyes never left mine. "This is how it was always meant to be. How it could have only ever have been. Looking into the past hoping things would be different is an act of insanity and will drive you mad as such."

"Not everyone believes that," I said, not sure what I believed at the moment.

"Then it is good for you and I that the Lord of the Way does not change on what some people or others do or do not believe." Enoch nodded as if he were content he had said enough. He extended his free hand. "Thank you."

"What will you do now?" I asked, accepting his hand.

"Our path is clear," Enoch answered. "We travel back to the cities and warn those there of the evil that is coming for them. If we can even get a few to listen, it will be worth it."

"Good luck," I said, releasing Enoch's hand.

"Luck has never been anything but an illusion," Enoch said with a grin before he turned and made his way to the waiting ship.

"So you gonna check out that chip Rose gave you or what?" Cryx asked, coming up to me. "She gave it to both of us, you know."

"You still tripping from your stim high?" I asked her sideways. "I'm pretty sure she gave it to me."

"What's on it?" Cryx asked.

"X?" I asked. "There a way you can access the information on this?"

"Yes," X answered. "I'll display the content in a holographic image in front of you."

"You'd be lost without her," Cryx said, eyeing X's chip behind my right ear.

"I tell her that all the time," I answered.

"Here we go," X said, ignoring the exchange.

A series of light blue numbers popped to life in front of me, followed by another list of what looked like addresses, company names, and listings.

"What are we looking at?" Cryx asked. "What is all of this?"

My eyes widened as I remembered what the old

woman had told me. She was wealthy, wanting to explore, when she accidentally stumbled on the Voy base.

Rose had been putting it lightly. She wasn't just wealthy, she was among the one percent on Mars. The listings were of bank accounts, balances, companies owned and assets.

There were bank accounts with more zeros in them than I cared to count.

"Holy crip," Cryx blurted as she also put the pieces of the puzzle together. "Are those bank accounts?"

"Yeah," I answered. "X, you can close it."

X turned off the information scrolling in front of us.

"Whoa, whoa, whoa," Cryx said, looking at me like I was crazy. "I didn't get to read all of that. Turn it back on. Half of that should be mine."

"Not a chance," I answered. "Rose didn't die for you to blow her money on drugs and partying."

The memory of Rose's death seemed to take the wind out of Cryx's sails. I knew it was harsh, but that was what she needed to hear at the moment.

"And you understand none of these credits matter in the slightest if we aren't around to use them," I said. "I'll give it to Enoch to look after. His people will need a place to stay once they're back in the city. You should go with them. Trade in your Hessian title for the Way maybe."

"Yeah, okay." Cryx rolled her eyes. "What in the history of our relationship would make you think I'd do that?"

"They're good people," I said, walking over to the ship that acted more as a human transport than supply craft now carrying everyone back to the cities.

Cryx followed.

"A place, funds to help you and your people get back on their feet," I told Enoch as I pressed the chip into his hand. "Look out for Cryx."

"Thank you," Enoch said, eyeing the chip in his hand with obvious wonder. "We will. She has a place with us. We will take care of your home until you return."

I just nodded. I didn't feel like going into the story of how it wasn't really my home, where it came from, or whose blood was still dried on the data chip.

"Hey," Cryx shouted as the sounds of the ship's thrusters fired up.

I turned around to look at her.

"Thanks" she said.

I nodded as I watched the ship make a giant U-turn inside the settlement walls then leave out the front gates.

Wesley Cage along with Angel and Jax were speaking outside of the open dropship's rear doors. A team of Immortal Corp scientists worked in excited glee as they went through the settlement collecting the bodies of the fallen Voy aliens.

I made my way over, wondering what I would say. A simple hello seemed much too out of place at this point.

"Daniel," Cage said with a nod. "I'm glad to see you whole."

"Good to be whole," I answered. I wasn't much for small talk. "Preacher, we need to get him back."

"And we will," Cage said. He pulled his signature cigar from his mouth after taking a long puff. Heck, I wasn't sure if it was the same one he always had or another identical smoke. I guess it didn't really matter. "We're sending in a scouting party tonight to watch the area where the Voy have set up shop. We'll go in as soon as we have a plan and an opening. In the meantime, we need to get you back to base and debrief. Anything you know might help us see Preacher safe again and end this war before it gets started."

"Where's this base?" I asked.

"We have our headquarters in Athens," Cage supplied. "We'll go there now. You know, even with you back, we're a bit short handed. With Echo, we'd stand a better chance."

"I'm not back and you know as much as I do about Echo," I told him. "You know more than I did. You knew he was sent to kill Amber."

Cage took another long puff of his cigar. The bright orange ember glowed against the light of the day.

"I found out once it had already happened," Cage said with a hard stare not directed at me but rather at the events of the past. "Not that it helps at all. I should have seen it coming. I was her handler in the field. I'm as much to blame for it as anyone."

"You couldn't have known," Jax said softly. "None of us did."

"You want Echo, you can go and grab him," I said with a shrug.

"No, I don't think Immortal Corp has the resources to fight a war on two fronts at the moment," Cage said. "We concentrate on getting Preacher back and stopping this alien invasion, then we'll see about freeing Echo."

That was fine with me. I had no love for Echo nor felt the need to offer info or details about Phoenix. As far as I was concerned, I was a free man allowed to set his own alliances. At the moment, I was only with Immortal Corp to free Preacher, see that the known galaxy didn't get overrun by aliens, and kill the founding members of Immortal Corp.

While the scientists did their sweep of the area, we followed Wesley Cage inside the dropship. The craft looked like all the others before with a cargo area in the rear and seats in the second half of the ship.

A tall woman with a pale complexion spoke with Wesley briefly, stealing glances in my direction. She wore a tight button-up suit that lined up on the left side of her body. Wesley told her something then came over to us.

"Doctor Bishop would like to begin the debriefing with you now," Cage asked, looking at each of us in turn. "If you're feeling up to it, feel free to recharge on food while we do so. I know the healing process for each of you takes a lot of calories to complete."

"Fine by me," Jax answered. "The faster we debrief, the faster we get back to Preacher."

"Count me in," Angel added.

"Me too," I said.

Wesley Cage waved the doctor over.

I wasn't sure how the doctor could even move. Her black suit was tight on her body, not leaving much to the imagination. She smiled at me, fidgeting with her datapad as she began in an accent I couldn't place, maybe Russian from the old world.

"Daniel Hunt, I have heard so much about you," Doctor Bishop began. She extended a gloved hand. "Doctor Chloe Bishop. I head the science department for Immortal Corp."

"Of course you do," I said, shaking her hand.

"I took over as head of the department in the time since you left. I had very much wanted to meet you after going over your reports and files but feared you wouldn't come back," the doctor said, releasing my hand and offering me a seat in the dropship. "Imagine my surprise and excitement when the fastest healing member of the infamous Pack Protocol had been found and was willing to come in."

"Imagine that," I said, going over to a seat and looking around for something to eat.

"Do you require something?" Doctor Bishop asked.

"You have anything to snack on around here?" I asked.

"Thomas!" the doctor screamed.

A short, balding man with glasses and similar black suit that buttoned up on the left side of the jacket appeared from the cockpit area of the ship.

"Mr. Hunt would like some victuals" Doctor Bishop ordered.

"At once," Thomas said. He moved to stand on top

of one of the seats and began rummaging through the overhead compartment.

"Thomas will see to it that you are well taken care of," Doctor Bishop took a seat right next to me.

Out of the many seats across and alongside me, she had to choose the one immediately next to me.

"Now please start at the beginning of what happened to you, the first thing that you remember once you woke up on the moon," Doctor Bishop asked. "We have time. It's a long ride to Athens."

I started from the beginning, telling her everything from my time as a gladiator throwing people out of bars to journeying to Earth and now here on Mars.

I glossed over some details, like seeing Sam and where she was. I had a sneaking suspicion Immortal Corp knew where she was hiding out, but I wasn't going to be the one to confirm that.

Things like the Voy took a lot longer and I made sure to divulge every little bit of information I could remember. X popped in and out of the conversation providing details.

We were at it for almost an hour.

The entire time, I ate protein bars and pre-made meal packs, replenishing the calories my body had lost healing itself.

The whole time, Doctor Bishop made notes,

nodding encouragingly. She spoke up only a few times, asking for clarification.

Immortal Corp scientists came in and out of the rear of the dropship loaded down with large zippered bags I knew held Voy bodies. They were really cleaning up out there. Anything not burned was bagged and tagged.

"And now I'm here waiting for this bird to take off so we can regroup and go get Preacher," I told the doctor. "That's about it."

"Very interesting," Doctor Bishop said, adjusting her glasses. "I wonder if—"

"Get down, hands in the air!"

Shouts from outside the dropship reached our ears. Wesley Cage was outside the dropship like a fire had been started under him. We all followed close behind.

What now? I asked myself. *Did we not kill one of them? Had one of the Voy somehow managed to stay alive?*

TWENTY-FIVE

"IT JUST APPEARED a few seconds ago, sir," one of the armored Immortal Corp soldiers told Cage as we arrived at the settlement's main gates. "It came out of nowhere."

We stood at the front entrance to the settlement. The gates were still open from when the supply craft had exited with the survivors.

A few hundred meters in front of us, some kind of cloaked ship had taken shape. Well, not the craft at all, but rather, a hatch was opened on the cloaked ship. We could see inside the invisible ship like a door had opened out of thin air.

The alien vessel had to be smaller than a dropship. From it exited a handful of Voy soldiers, Dall, and Preacher.

All around me, Immortal Corp soldiers tensed. I heard Doctor Bishop suck in a long draw of breath as they saw live aliens for the first time.

Dall dragged Preacher toward us over the sand. Preacher was bloody. He didn't move at all.

"I have come to return your animal," Dall shouted at us. He threw Preacher in front of him. "Before you insist on doing anything rash, know that the cloaked ship behind me is one of our smaller fighter vessels. My pilot has the heavy weapons aimed at you now. A move against us would result in the death of all of you right now."

I felt the flow of adrenaline hit me. I was ready to go right then, despite the warning.

"Why tell us that at all?" Cage asked, removing the ever present cigar from his mouth. "Why not just kill us? You took us by surprise. You know that."

"Mmm, a clever human," Dall said with a crooked grin. "I need you to deliver a message for me."

"And that would be?" Cage asked.

"Your race is ordered to submit to Voy rule," Dall answered. "You have seven days to comply. If you have not done so in seven days, three-quarters of your population will be destroyed. The rest will be taken by force and employed by the Voy empire as we see fit."

"You say employ and I think you really mean

enslaved," I retorted. I couldn't help myself. "Seven days isn't enough time to get an entire species on the same page."

"Not my concern," Dall said, looking down at the heap in front of him that was Preacher's body. "I've also brought back your friend as proof that we are not scared of your kind. Not even the strongest among you will be able to stand against us now."

The wicked smile on his lips told me something was very wrong. The way Preacher didn't move at all confirmed it.

Dall moved forward, kicking Preacher over on his back. The Voy placed a foot on Preacher's neck.

Angel stepped forward, her free hand going to the blaster at her side.

Cage lifted a hand in her direction to stop her.

"You've made your point," Cage called out to Dall. "We'll deliver your message."

"May this image serve as a reminder to you," Dall said, grinning down at the helpless form of Preacher. "In seven days, we will stand on the necks of humanity. One way or the other."

With that, Dall turned and walked back into the ship. The contingent of Voy soldiers followed him into the doorway that seemed to appear out of thin air. The door closed, and a second later, a low whine of thrusters filled the air. Sand was whipped about and they were gone.

I sprinted to Preacher's side, reaching him at the same time as Jax and Angel.

"Oh, what did they do to you?" Angel said, skidding to her knees. "What did they do to you?"

Preacher was a mess. That meant a lot coming from me. They had taken off his eye patch, leaving his empty eye socket to stare up at the sky. His one good eye was swollen shut. They had worked him over pretty well. His body was a mass of cuts and bruises that as far as I could tell weren't healing.

He moved his mouth to try to say something, but only a grimace twisted his bloody lips.

"There's something wrong," Jax said, leaning over his body. "He should be healing. These wounds look older. Infection is already starting to set in."

Cage finally caught up to us.

His eyes were hard. If he had been shocked to see the aliens, he didn't show it.

"Let's get him on the dropship," Cage said, looking over at Doctor Bishop, who also arrived, panting for breath. "Can you help him?"

Doctor Bishop tapped a few buttons on her datapad. A dark blue light came from her pad, scanning the unmoving Preacher.

"Internal bleeding, broken bones, bruising, and lacerations across his body." Doctor Bishop shook her head. "I don't understand. He should be able to have healed from most if not all of these wounds. I mean, at least be in the process of healing. I need to take a closer look."

"Let's go." I scooped Preacher up as gently as I could. He wasn't a little man, but right now, he felt as fragile as a newborn. "Hang in there."

We ran back to the dropship. My arms and legs burned by the time we got him inside. Thomas and Doctor Bishop set up a gurney for Preacher and went to work connecting needles and IV's to him, monitors and holographic displays with readouts I didn't understand.

I felt helpless as I stood by and watched. For all my unnatural ability and knowledge, I was useless when it came to helping now. Apparently, I wasn't the only one who felt this way.

Angel slammed a fist into the side of the dropship so hard, it made an indentation. She stalked out of the rear hatch.

Jax caught my eye.

"She just needs some time," Jax said, nodding with his chin over to Preacher's prone form. "He's like a dad to her. To a lot of us. I think that's why Immortal

Corp chose him. Six young pups and an older wolf to lead us."

Cage walked back into the dropship, his face a mask of stern displeasure.

"We need to get going," he said, looking at Jax and me. "Orders are to head back to base. We can get Preacher better help there, start dissecting these things, and reassemble. Jax, I need your muscles helping to get the last of these aliens inside the dropship. Wheels up in ten."

"Angel," Jax said, looking at me with a nod. "Go get her."

"I'm not really one for talking nice to people and making them feel better," I said, shying away from the responsibility. "Maybe I could help load the bodies and you get her."

"No such luck," Jax said, leaving with Cage. "You're on deck."

I watched the two men leave, not really sure what I would say to Angel to make her feel better.

X sensed my hesitancy.

"So are you going to go talk to her or what?" X asked. "She's just a person hurting right now. One of your friends. Or at least someone who used to be a friend."

"I don't know what to say to make her feel better,"

I answered. "What am I supposed to do? Promise her that everything will be okay when I have no idea if that's even the truth?"

"Sometimes you don't have to say anything," X answered. "Sometimes just being there is enough."

I scratched the back of my head, preferring to stare down a squad of Voy soldiers rather than try to have a talk that involved feelings and emotion.

I looked over at the other side of the dropship where Preacher lay sucking in oxygen with the help of a mask Doctor Bishop had placed over his mouth and nose.

There wasn't anything I could do for him at the moment, but maybe there was something I could do for Angel.

I walked from the rear of the Immortal Corp dropship out onto the settlement grounds. The scientist team had done an amazing job in a short amount of time. The last Voy bodies were being loaded aboard the dropship. The only things that remained at all to speak of the fight that had taken place here were the scorch marks from blaster fire on the buildings themselves.

All the alien weaponry had also been confiscated.

I found Angel on the catwalk. She stared out into the distance. Her dark hair was pulled behind her, her muscular arms crossed over her chest. She looked pissed.

I decided to take X's advice. I didn't say a word. I just stood beside her and stared out into the Martian landscape. Red sand and rolling dunes stretched out as far as I could see in every direction.

The smell of death was still on the air.

"You think he's going to make it?" Angel asked without looking at me. "Whatever they did to him stopped his ability to heal, that much seems obvious."

"If the same spirit that lives inside of you and me lives inside Preacher, then, yeah, he's going to make it," I said, not looking at her either. "I know he will."

"How can you be so sure?" Angel asked. "You got faith or something now? Enoch rub off on you?"

"No—I mean, maybe. I don't know." I said. "Preacher's a fighter. He'll pull through."

"I'm going to tear those Voy apart with my hands and teeth," Angel said, not trying to hide the hate in her voice. "Even if they have figured out a way to stop our abilities, that's not going to save them."

"I'm with you," I told her.

Angel turned to look at me for the first time in the conversation.

"The vendetta you have against Immortal Corp? I

mean, for what they did to Amber. What happens to that?" Angel asked.

"It's still there," I said. "I'll never work for the company again. The two founders who gave the kill order are still targets, but I understand that needs to be put on hold for the time being. I can't take my vengeance if they're not here to take it out on."

"I'm glad you're back," Angel said with a grim nod. "We'll need you."

TWENTY-SIX

THE RIDE to the city of Athens on Mars was short. At least it seemed like it was. I slept most of the way.

Doctor Bishop informed us that Preacher was stabilized, but his healing ability had indeed been neutralized somehow. Whether this was temporary or permanent was yet to be seen.

Before the doctor could get us anything definite, she needed access to her equipment back at the company's headquarters.

When we finally touched down in Athens, it was dark. I was roused by the shudder of the dropship as it landed. Preacher was rushed off with the doctor for immediate care.

Cage oversaw the scientists as they unloaded the alien corpses.

"Shower, rest more if you can, and eat," Cage told us. "We'll have a meeting with next steps soon."

Despite having seen the aliens himself and knowing that they were only days from waging their war, Cage seemed as cool as a poker player with a winning hand.

"Does anything every rattle that guy?" I asked, following Jax and Angel as we prepared to leave the dropship.

"If anything does, we haven't discovered it yet," Jax answered.

The dropship had landed on a high rise building. Cold wind whipped around my head, sending a chill down my spine. The building we landed on had to be twenty, maybe thirty stories tall.

Armed guards waited for us, ushering us into a grand entrance with tall doors. The ground sloped down and I found myself in a hall with a series of lifts on the left and right.

"Bring back any memories?" Angel asked.

"No, not yet," I said trying to will myself to remember more.

"Maybe once you see your old room," Jax said, going over to a lift and pressing his hand in a square indentation in the wall. The pad went from red to green. The doors slid open from the middle, granting us access to the lift.

We entered the large square compartment.

Angel seemed to be doing better now that Preacher was stabilized. A cold fury still lived behind her eyes, but she kept it together.

The door slid closed and Jax pressed a button for the fifteenth floor.

"We kept your room just like you left it," Jax said. "I'm down the hall on your left and Angel is on the right if you need anything."

"Thanks," I said.

The doors dinged open. We were led into another wide hall. A grey metal floor, walls, and ceiling greeted us. Bright lights clicked on down the hall, turning on in a domino kind of effect as sensors reacted to our presence.

The doors on either side of the hall were offset. Each doorway was a wide archway.

"Farther down the hall is the cafeteria if you get hungry," Jax said as he and Angel stopped by a door. "This is you."

I stood in front of the tall arched door for a moment.

For a long time, this is what you wanted, a home, answers,

I thought to myself. *Now that you have both, things aren't simpler, just more complicated than ever.*

"We'll leave you to it," Angel said as she and Jax left me in front of my door.

"Thanks," I said absently.

A square indentation just like the one on the lift was set into the right side of my door. I lifted my hand to press it to the metal then pulled it back before I made contact.

I felt a sense of dread in the pit of my stomach.

What if I didn't like who I was? What if this was a mistake?

"X, you there?" I asked, already knowing the answer. I just needed to buy more time before I stepped inside.

"Always," X responded. "Are you okay?"

"There's a long, complicated answer to that question," I said. "Probably not is the short version."

"Don't I know it," X teased me. "Are you going to go in?"

"I guess so," I said. "Just taking my time. I have a feeling that whatever's in the room is going to give me answers to my past I might not want to remember."

"More painful memories," X said for me. "We don't have to. We can request a new room for you."

"But I'd rather know," I said. "At least, right now, I think I would rather know."

"Things change, Daniel," X said. "Your plan to kill the founders of Immortal Corp. Is that still a go?"

"The anger I hold for them is still there, just taken a back seat to the invasion on our hands," I mused out loud. "But maybe it's for the better. Maybe it's good to come back. Lull them into a sense of security before chopping the head off the snake."

"Perhaps," X said. "Be careful, Daniel. You're in a game now where all the players are still not known."

"Oh, you know me," I said.

"Yes, I do," X agreed. "Hence the warning."

I took a deep breath. My mouth was dry.

I placed my palm against the cool metal hand reader next to my door. It shone red then green. Something clicked inside the door and the doors slid open.

The wall lights blinked on in my room.

It smelled kind of musty, like no one had used it in a number of years. I took a tentative step inside. It was clean and simple. A bed on the left with a closet beside it. A chest on the floor by the bed and a desk with a chair on the opposite side of the room.

Windows looking out onto the city were placed in the wall next to the bed. Some kind of whiteboard was nailed to the wall just beside the desk. I took all of this in, in an instant.

My eyes were pulled to two pictures that sat in shallow shelves above my desk. In one, I was dressed up with Amber beside me. We looked happy. She looked amazing. Despite the image, I couldn't remember why we were there. Was it a wedding? Some kind of celebration?

I didn't know.

The next picture was just of her. That smile on her face as if it lived inside of her and the joy just pushed its way out. In that picture, she was in a field somewhere, with a bright blue sky behind her. Again, I didn't remember where it had been taken.

I couldn't tell if I was happy, sad, or angry. Her face brought a smile to my own. Sadness for not being able to hold her ever again and anger for her being murdered filled my heart.

Moving to the windows in the room, I looked out over the still sleeping city of Athens. Unlike Elysium, this city seemed far more business-oriented, at least this section of the city did.

Elysium was statues and fountains, wide streets, one- to two-story buildings, and a sense of leisure. Athens, with its tall business buildings and lack of any artistic flair I could see, felt colder.

"Daniel," X said. "I know you're dealing with a lot right now, but we have an incoming transmission."

"The Order?" I asked, hopeful.

"Captain Valentine," X answered.

I didn't know I was so eager to hear back from the masked Cyber Hunter until that moment. I hoped my transmission to her had gone through. Something told me we would need the help of the Order before this was all over.

"Go ahead, I'm good," I lied. "Put her through."

"Daniel are you there?" Captain Valentine asked.

"Yeah, yeah, I'm here," I answered.

"Seems like you may not be so insane after all," she said. "At least not about this one."

"You got someone to listen?" I asked.

"That major who owed me a favor took a look at the images you sent. Things didn't sound promising at first, but a supply craft with members of a Way settlement rolled into town with a story about being attacked by aliens," Captain Valentine said, pausing here. "As luck would have it, the major has known this Way leader for a long time. It was enough to make him listen."

Atta boy, Enoch, I said to myself.

"They'll go check it out?" I asked. "I mean, not the Way settlement. That place has been picked dry by

Immortal Corp. They need to head to the coordinates I sent you and tell them to stay out of sight. The place is cloaked. They'll have to use heat signature vision pumped up at a hundred times the normal power to see them."

"I said he'll listen," the captain corrected me. "Before the Galactic Government commits resources to this, they want harder evidence. I can't believe I'm saying this, but if you—if you have that alien body with you, you should bring it in."

"I will," I answered. "Where? When?"

"The major is putting a request in to get me to Athens immediately," Captain Valentine answered. "I'll be there tomorrow. Meet me at the Hall of Power tomorrow night."

"We need to hurry," I said, remembering the timeline Dall put on the invasion. "We have seven days before they attack. Their message is to submit and be enslaved. If we refuse, they promise to wipe out three-quarters of the human population and then take the rest as prisoners."

The line on the other end was silent.

"Zoe, are you there?" I asked.

"Yeah—yeah, I'm here," Zoe said. "I just still can't believe this. Part of me is still hoping that you're nuts.

You had too many concussions or something and that you belong in a mental institution. No offense."

"None taken," I answered. "I wish I was nuts as well. It would be an easier fix than going to war."

"Tomorrow night, Hall of Power in Athens." Captain Valentine repeated the location. "Eight o'clock, don't be late."

"I'll see you then," I answered.

The transmission ended.

"You think Immortal Corp is going to let you take one of the Voy specimens and walk right into the Hall of Power to hand it over to the GG?" X asked.

"I don't know," I said. "I guess we'll find out soon. On second thought, I think they will. I hope they're smart enough to understand what we're up against here."

"I hope you're right," X answered with a shudder in her voice. "I hope you're right."

TWENTY-SEVEN

DESPITE BEING IN A NEW ENVIRONMENT, when my head hit the pillow, I was out like a light. Maybe it was something about being in a place I had called home for ten years. Maybe I was just that dog tired. But after a hot shower, I was out cold.

When most dreams hit, I knew somewhere in the back of my mind that what I was experiencing wasn't real. Somewhere deep down, I knew this was taking place in the theater of the mind, but it felt so real.

I stood on a sharp mountain peak. All around me, dark night covered the sky like a blanket. Thousands of stars and planets filled the night like they had been sprinkled there, each one taking a very specific place in the dark sky.

The stars weren't alone; planets dotted the landscape as well. I had a zoomed-in vision to the galaxy around me.

My hair stood on end when I realized I wasn't alone. On the bleak mountain peak, a tall woman walked toward me. She was older and maybe I should have been afraid, but there was a wisdom in her eyes that told me everything was going to be okay.

She wore a long white dress, with jewels on her slender neck, wrists, and fingers.

I didn't think I was in danger, but I had not been trained to think. I was conditioned to be prepared for anything. My hand dropped to my right thigh where my MK II should have been.

It was gone.

"You don't need to fear me," the woman said in a light, almost happy tone. "Not me, Daniel Hunt."

"Who are you? How do you know my name?" I asked.

"Of all the questions you should be asking right now, those are not the two I would suggest," the woman said, looking up into our enhanced view of the galaxy. "But I will humor you. You've been through a lot and still have the hardest part of your journey in front of you. I'm a friend. That's all you need to know for now. I know your name because you alone stand at a crossroads that would see the human race defended or defeated."

"Are you a Voy?" I asked. The woman looked human enough to me, but who knew what they could or couldn't do. Maybe they could change form. "If not a Voy, then you're an alien for sure."

"I do not descend from the Voy species." The woman gave me a motherly-looking gaze.

I withered underneath it. Suddenly, I was a little kid again, receiving a disapproving look from a teacher.

"Enough about who or what I am. I have come to help," she said, motioning to the sky above us with an open hand. "Your species sent out a beacon when they cultivated the moon and Mars. Unbeknownst to them, the galaxy turned their attention to your kind when they realized you were beginning to claim moons and planets as your own. The Voy saw this as an opportunity to enslave such an industrious species. Other species sit and wait to see what will happen while still others are planning to infiltrate your Earth and set up new homes."

"Other species." I repeated the words with a sigh. "How many other species are we talking about?"

"How many stars are in the sky?" the woman said with a tired grin. "In your galaxy alone, there are hundreds. Across the universe, there could be thousands, maybe even more."

"This isn't my fight," I said, shaking my head. "I have my hands full enough with the Voy and my own personal problems. I can't police the Earth."

"You are correct," the woman agreed. "You should not have to bear this burden alone. You will need others to stand by you. If you succeed in repelling the Voy, a new, what you call corporation will have to rise, one to fight the battles regular humans can't."

"You have any good news in any of this?" I asked with a sigh. "Fight off the Voy only to fight off other alien species."

"To whom much is given, much is asked," the woman answered. "You have a choice in this. There is always a choice. Even now you can turn your back on humanity and walk away. No one is forcing you to stand against the Voy."

"You know I can't turn back now," I said. "There's no real choice here. I sit this one out, humankind dies."

"Maybe," the woman said. "Know that not all species that exist in your galaxy would see you fall. There are those who will give aid. Others are waiting to see if humankind is the species they hope it is before stepping in. Think of this battle with the Voy as a kind of test. This is humanity's first trial run at defending themselves."

"Some test," I said. "Lose and die."

"It's a cold place out there." The woman tilted her head up to take in the stars and planets around us. "But you'll make it. The only way you won't is if you give up. You don't strike me as the kind to give up."

"What is it that you want?" I asked.

The woman looked at me with a raised eyebrow.

"They always want something," I said. "You're here out of the goodness of your heart? I'm just going to put two and two together here. You're an alien who has a vested interest in humankind defeating the Voy. Because why? You need them taken out?"

For the first time, I saw anger flash in her eyes. I had faced down my fair share of Voy, a Cyber Hunter, and mercenaries. None of them gave me the sense of dread from the inside out like her stare.

"You would be wise in choosing your words when you speak to me, human. I could kill you now in your mind's eye." She took a deep breath, restraining herself. "You're right. I do have a vested interest in seeing humanity succeed. Not all of us are as evil as you might think. I see that humanity is capable of great things if they can just get out of their own way. If you can weather this storm, you will let the galaxy know you are not to be taken lightly."

"Great, so why don't you just come in with your own alien friends and military and give us a hand?" I asked.

"That is not my path or my battle to fight," she said. "I have another calling. My way is clear."

I heaved a heavy sigh, looking up into the night sky.

"So kill the Voy and be ready for other aliens to infiltrate Earth," I said with a shrug. "Is that the gist of your visit?"

"That warning and to tell you that you are not alone. You never have been." The woman turned to go. "You are the key, Daniel. You hold the necessary rela-tionships to unite humankind whether you see that now or not. I really should be going. She's been waiting to speak with you and so patient, I might add."

"Who, who are you talking about?" I asked the back of the woman as she dissipated into the night.

"Me." X's voice sounded not in my head like it usually did but beside me.

I turned to my left to see a smiling X in her human body. Her short black hair and skin tight blue suit were how she took on physical manifestation.

"I couldn't appear for some reason," X said. "At

least not while the woman was here. I heard everything, but it was like she was asking me to wait until
she was finished."

"Can you tell who or what she was?" I asked.

"Nope, I know as much as you do," X answered. "I
know she's powerful on a cerebral level. It's a power I
don't yet understand. Nothing like what we have on
Earth. I would use the word 'magic' but that's just a
term used for science we can't comprehend."

"It's good to see you, X," I said.

"It's good to be seen," X answered.

"So what do you make out of all of this?" I asked,
looking up to the light show in the night sky. "You
think we have a chance of defeating the Voy? You think
she was telling the truth about other species infil-
trating Earth?"

"I don't see a reason for her to lie," X said, taking a
seat and drawing her knees to her chest. She wrapped
her arms around both limbs. "All she did was warn you
and encourage you. I do think we can defeat the Voy. It
makes sense that other species would infiltrate Earth.
Think who's on there now."

"What do you mean?" I asked.

"I mean, Earth is pretty much an empty house," X
answered. "I know it's a dead planet, but with so few
people living there now, what's stopping aliens from

going in and setting up shop? Who knows? They might not even all be bad. Maybe some just need a home."

"You're making them sound like victims here," I said.

"Maybe some of them are, maybe not." X shrugged. "I guess you and whatever corporation you set up will have to figure that out case by case."

"Whoa, whoa, whoa," I said, pushing my hands out in front of me. "Pump the brakes. Let's deal with this Voy invasion and Immortal Corp first before we start talking about setting up our own company."

I took a seat beside a silent X and we stared up at the stars together.

"We'll figure it all out," X said after a brief pause. "We always do."

X put her head on my shoulder a moment later and fell asleep.

KNOCKING at the door woke me in the morning.

It was Jax.

"Hey, we have a meeting and an update on Preacher." Jax sounded happy. "He's going to pull through.

It'll take time, but he's going to be okay. If you hurry, we can go see him now before the meeting happens."

I sat up, wiping a line of drool from the right corner of my mouth. It was the first piece of good news we had had in awhile. Memories of my dream gave me both hope and worry at once. I decided not to tell anyone for the time being.

What would I say anyway? That I was visited by a possible powerful alien race who told me I was the key to all of this and that if we defeat the Voy to watch out because rogue aliens will be setting up shop on Earth? That sounded crazy in my own mind and I had heard some pretty wild stuff lately.

"You're wearing clothes, right? Don't sleep in the nude or anything weird?" Jax asked.

"I'm good, you can come in," I said, walking over to the door and pressing the pad to let Jax in.

Jax entered the room with a tray holding a steaming pile of breakfast on one end and folded clothes on the other.

The smell of strong caf and the breakfast set me drooling again. The clothing he brought in with him lifted the corner of my lip in a growl.

I recognized the black uniform. Heavy boots and cargo pants with a tight-fitting shirt. An emblem of a snarling wolf on the left sleeve confirmed the Immortal Corp uniform.

Jax wore it himself. The clothing was flat black just like the armor we would wear when going out on missions. I remembered that much now. I guess some of my memories were coming back.

"Dress and let's eat on the go," Jax said, looking around my room with a smile. "It's good to see you back in your old room. I haven't been in here since you left. How'd you sleep?"

"Like a dead man," I answered, pulling on the pants and boots. I guess it wasn't that much of a lie. I had slept well despite the vivid dream. "Angel good to go?"

"She's not a morning person, but she popped out of bed when I told her about Preacher," Jax answered. "She's with him now. Her healing ability has her at nearly a hundred percent."

I pulled the black shirt over my head as a thought came to mind. The black gear made me think of a memory that was just out of reach.

"You can wear any color as long as it's black," I said out loud.

Jax laughed. It was a deep real chuckle from the big man.

"Preacher would say that all the time when we

geared up to go out on a mission," Jax said, tugging at his black beard. "I think it was Sam that asked if we could have grey or olive uniforms. It became a running joke."

Jax's memory of the event turned from joy to sadness. I could only guess at what he was remembering. How Sam was no longer part of the Pack Protocol or how Amber was dead. Maybe that Echo was gone now as well.

"All right big man," I said grabbing the steaming cup of caf and the hot plate of delicious-looking food. "Lead the way."

TWENTY-EIGHT

I WALKED and ate while Jax did the talking. We made our way back to the lifts and lower level Jax called the med wing.

When the doors opened, we were greeted with white floors and ceilings. There were walls, but they were made of glass. I saw empty hospital beds, doctors, and lab technicians going over reports and working at holographic monitor stations.

Toward the end of the hall, Jax made a hard right. A room with fogged glass stood in front of us. The door was open. Inside, Preacher lay propped up on a white linen bed. Tubes ran out of his arms and neck. The swelling on his face had gone down a bit.

A metal patch with no band around it covered his missing eye. He was awake when we walked in.

Angel sat next to him on a stool.

"Sorry we're late to the party," Jax said, grabbing a chair. He grinned at Preacher. "Glad to see you awake and functioning, Alpha Wolf."

"Good to be aware of what's going on around me," Preacher said. "I blacked out for a long stretch."

"Thank you for what you did back there," I told him. "You bought us the time we needed to escape. All of us."

I felt a tinge of regret at having left him at all. The plan was to go back for him, but obviously, we were too late. The deed had been done.

"Any of you would have done it if you were in my place," Preacher said with a shrug. The simple act seemed to bring a heavy pain to his chest. He winced. "No use not addressing the dropship in the room. Whatever the Voy did to me, they were able to neutralize my healing ability. I'm a message more than anything else. They can kill us. They can kill the strongest we can send against them."

"How?" I asked. "How did they do it?"

"They put a bug in me because they thought that might soften me up." Preacher grinned through a split lip. "When that didn't work, they took some bone marrow samples, created some kind of injection that nullified my healing ability. There's a more technical explanation of course, but you'll have to talk to Doctor Bishop on that one."

"Is the—is the process permanent?" Angel asked.

"It's too soon to tell," Preacher said, refusing to let the idea that he had lost his ability entered his mind. "No sense in worrying about that now. The scientists and doctors are on it. I'll be fine. Even without my healing ability, I'll be back on my feet sooner or later. It's up to you three to do what needs to be done. You stay on point."

"The Voy are going to pay," Jax said, flexing his hands. "When I get my hands on them, I promise they'll pay."

"You watch each other's backs out there," Preacher told us. "Cage said the Voy are coming in seven days. I'll be with you when it all goes down. Even if they haven't fixed my ability to heal, so help me God, I'll be there. I owe the Voy a debt. They just killed my body. They haven't killed my spirit."

The look of raw determination in Preacher's one good eye told me all I needed to know. He might be older, but he was just as crazy as the rest of us. He would be on the frontlines with us in a wheelchair if that was what it took. I had no doubt about that.

"You two mind if I have a talk with Daniel alone?"

Preacher asked Jax and Angel. "I need to tell him something."

"Sure," Jax said, moving to leave the room.

"We'll be back to check in on you soon," Angel said, giving Preacher a gentle squeeze to his hand.

The two left the room, closing the door behind them.

I had no idea what Preacher wanted to talk to me about. It could be about my reappearance, my role now in the Pack, or something else entirely.

"I did it, Danny," Preacher confessed, swallowing hard. "I need you to know that. When they killed Amber without any of us the wiser, I took you out to save you."

My mind exploded in a dozen different directions at once. One of the main parts of the missing puzzle was finally being filled in.

"I knew you'd retaliate right away and they'd kill you too," Preacher explained. "It was the only way to keep you safe. I couldn't lose—I couldn't lose you too."

Anger, confusion, and tears of frustration sprang to my eyes.

A lone tear fell down Preacher's one good eye, but for a completely different reason.

"Why didn't you tell me sooner?" I couldn't help

but yell. Adrenaline pumped free through my veins and I wasn't sure if I wanted to hit the wall or Preacher at the moment.

"Fear, if I'm being honest," Preacher admitted. If he was ashamed of letting the tears fall in front of me, he didn't show it. "I didn't want you to turn your back on the pack for my mistake. When Amber was taken out—"

"You can just say it how it is," I interrupted. "When Immortal Corp ordered Amber murdered."

"When Immortal Corp ordered Amber murdered," Preacher forced himself to say. "I heard about it from Cage first. I had to act then or not at all. I found you, gassed you, wiped your mind, and dropped you on the moon. I can see the error of my ways now, but at the time, in that split second, I had to make the decision before you found out. It was the best thing I could come up with. I wanted something better for you, Danny. I don't know if you can believe me or forgive me, but I wanted you to be free from all of this."

There was a battle raging inside of me. On one hand, he was right. If I knew what happened to her, I would have gone straight for the Immortal Corp founders and ripped their throats out. At least, I would have tried to. I can't imagine in that state going about it as tactfully as I was now. I would have rushed in in a fit of rage and more than likely gotten myself killed.

Preacher saved me then and he saved me again, leaving the Voy compound.

On the other hand, he had wiped my memory, basically kidnapped me, and left me in a gutter on the moon.

I wanted to kill him and hug him at the same time.

"You do what you got to do," Preacher said, holding my gaze. "I've made a lot of mistakes in my time. Saving you from yourself might have been one of them, but maybe not. I guess we'll never know how it would have played out if I didn't do anything."

"You could have told me before, when you saw me with Phoenix at the Immortal Corp safe house," I managed to say past my rage of confusion. "You could have told me so many times, but you didn't. You waited until now."

"More mistakes," Preacher admitted. "I couldn't drop it all on you at once. We have aliens at our doorstep and I'm the one responsible for your loss of memory? No, I couldn't. I stand behind that as the right decision."

I shook in frustration. Heat gathered in my face. How was I supposed to act? How was I supposed to respond? My hands clenched into fists and out again.

Instead of more words, I just left. I didn't trust myself not to say something I'd regret. I felt suffocated. I needed to breathe.

I stalked out of the room, slamming the door behind me. It was a kid thing to do, but it felt good. I turned the corner on my way back to the lift.

Angel sat on the floor with a flask to her lips. She looked up at me, handing it in my direction.

"Thought you might need a drink or twenty after Preacher talked to you," Angel said. "It's the good stuff. It'll make hair grow on your chest."

"You knew?" I asked, making no effort to accept the offered flask. "You knew and didn't say anything? You knew he was the one who wiped my memory?"

"Not until now." Angel shrugged, taking another long pull on the steel flask. "I had my suspicions, don't get me wrong. My money was on either Preacher or Cage. You sure you don't want any?"

"No, we can't get drunk anyway. Our metabolism processes the alcohol too fast," I growled.

"Speak for yourself," Angel said with a grin. "You have the fastest metabolism of all of us. I can still get a little buzz if I chug the stuff. It's a special blend. They call it Fire Water. I get it made special from some guys I know on the moon. It acts as fuel for vehicles too. Fun fact."

I could smell the stuff on her breath. I had no doubt it could fuel a dropship in a pinch.

"Is this how you deal with things?" I asked with a raised eyebrow. "Drowning your problems? I have news for you, sister. No amount of alcohol is going to clean our slate. My memory's still coming back and even I understand that. "

"A clean slate was never an option," Angel said, tilting her head completely back and draining her flask in long, hard chugs. She smacked her lips when she was done. "I don't drink on the job. Just before and after the missions. Sometime before bed, it helps with the nightmares."

I thought about it. We all had our issues and ways to cope. I guess none of us were innocent. Preacher lived in regret. Echo was insane. Jax was always fearful he wouldn't return to his normal state when he shifted. Sam was the closest to finding redemption, but even then, her past life was constantly called into action as she defended her small town.

"Nobody gets out of this life without scars. Nobody," Angel said with a belch that echoed down the hall. "Well, come on, help a girl to her feet. We're supposed to head to a meeting for orders."

Despite myself, I accepted her offered hand. She

rose to her feet, and to my surprise, was actually able to walk in a straight line.

We made our way to the lift.

Angel sighed disappointedly. "Already wearing off. I knew I should have brought the whole bottle."

TWENTY-NINE

THE BRIEFING ROOM was on a higher floor and didn't resemble either our barracks level or the med wing. This floor was black marble. The meeting room was long with an oval table and high-backed black chairs. On the far side of the room rested three blank screens.

My jaw twinged as I remembered the three screens in Echo's memory. This was where the Founders of Immortal Corp would appear to speak with us.

So close yet so far, I thought to myself. *Patience, their time will come.*

In the room, Jax and Cage already waited. Cage puffed a cigar, going over a datapad in his hands. Jax lounged deep in his chair.

"Glad you two could make it." Jax looked over at me. "You good?"

"Never better," I lied.

There was no point in keeping my interaction with Captain Valentine and the GG a secret. As I saw it, we needed all the help we could get and I doubted Immortal Corp would say no to the aid of the Galactic Government.

"I have a meeting with the GG tomorrow night," I told Cage. "They need proof. They want to see an alien body."

"I suspected as much," Cage said, looking up from the printouts scrolling across his screen. "I'm good with that. You going to be okay talking to the Founders?"

I knew exactly what he meant and everything he wasn't saying.

Well, are you? I asked myself. *Are you going to lose your crip as soon as their shadowed faces appear on the screens or can you hold it together long enough to find out who and where they are?*

I guessed time would tell. I didn't have a clear answer.

"Yeah, we've got bigger fish to fry," I told Cage.

"Good." Cage gave me a measured stare then went back to his datapad. "You know, it would help if we had Echo back. We're down a man with Preacher out for the count."

"Yeah, good luck with that," I said, choosing a chair across from Jax.

The three screens flickered, then were brought to life. In each image, a dark table with the silhouette of a person sitting at it appeared. Behind them, a dark green glow prevented us from seeing anything else.

I had seen the Founders before in Echo's memory. They looked the same. I guess that wasn't saying much, since I could only see their silhouettes. A bulkier man on the right I remembered as having a deep voice. A slender woman who acted as the leader in the middle and a silent man on the left.

"Daniel," the woman spoke with something like sincere joy in her voice. "It's so good to see you."

It took everything in me to nod and smile. I hoped they couldn't see through the charade.

"It's good to be back," I lied.

The woman seemed content with that. Neither of the men said anything.

"We've read the reports and we are aware of the situation," the man with the deep voice began. "Seven days isn't a whole lot. It's going to take everything Immortal Corp has built over the years to hold this invasion back, but we'll hold them."

I felt my heart rate quicken. Anger was boiling over

as they began talking about the alien invasion and how best to combat it.

There was no mention of Amber, what happened to me over the years, or why they had to kill her.

Did they think I didn't know? Did they think I was some puppet who was just going to fall in line again?

"Daniel," X said in my head. "Your heart rate is spiking. You know I'm with you no matter what. But you have the best chance of getting to the Founders if you play it cool here. An outburst is only going to set them on edge."

I knew X was right. I knew I should listen, but I just couldn't help myself.

"Daniel has an in with the Galactic Government that should prove useful," Cage was saying when I checked back into the conversation. "We need all the help we can get."

"That will be useful," the woman on the screen said. "We also have our inside people in the GG. We can ensure that the meeting will go our way and solidify their support. Daniel can be the mouthpiece for Immortal Corp."

"We'd have even more help than we needed if you didn't kill off our own," I said, hating the fact that I couldn't hold my tongue. At the same time, it felt great to identify the elephant in the room. "Maybe if you had listened to Amber, we could have the Order fighting alongside us as well."

The room went quiet. I could hear my heart drum in my ears.

Out of my peripheral vision, I could see Jax and Angel looking at me with wide eyes. Cage just took another puff of his cigar like he had expected this to happen the entire time.

"The Order has been our enemy since our inception," the woman said, never letting her voice rise or fall showing any kind of emotion. "I know you were close to her, but it was necessary."

"Can we count on you going forward?" the man with the deep voice asked, leaning into the screen. "Or do you need time to get over this?"

I didn't know what he meant about time, but I could guess he was hinting at killing me as well. The moment was charged for violence. I could feel it. We were a few exchanges from having the Founders order me taken in or killed.

I'd like to think that everyone in the room would have my back, but what about the other Immortal Corp soldiers in the building? What about them? I could fight my way out of here, but then what?

"Tell him," the silent man on the left said. It was

the first time I had heard his voice in Echo's memory or this conversation.

The other two Founders went silent. It was as if they respected this man. They had acted as the mouth-pieces, but this man, this man was the true leader behind the Founders.

"Are you sure?" the woman asked. "Things are complicated enough."

"Tell him," the man said again.

"Amber—Amber isn't dead," the woman in the screen told me.

My lower jaw fell open. Synapses fired in my brain, trying to make sense of the words coming out of her mouth. Was she lying? I had seen Amber die. At least I had seen it in Echo's memory.

"You're lying," I said, rising from my seat. I didn't know how that was going to help the situation, but it felt like the right thing to do. "I saw it."

"Then you saw wrong." The man with the deep voice actually sounded like he was enjoying the moment. "Echo did his best to kill Amber, but against all odds, she was taken."

"Taken?" Jax asked, just as confused as I was.

"What happened to her?" Angel asked. "Where is she?"

Cage didn't say anything, but I noticed he put his cigar down in an ashtray.

"How!" I slammed my fist down on the table.

I wasn't sure if it was all the shouting or if somehow one of the Founders had triggered a warning, but four Immortal Corp guards rushed into the room.

They wore matching black uniforms. No face protection, which was a huge mistake if they were going to try anything. In their hands, they carried batons that sparked with some kind of electric current.

"Calm yourself," the woman said.

"Or we'll calm you," the man with the deep voice followed.

I was actually happy to see the four guards rush into the room. I needed somewhere to vent my anger. I felt a twinge of guilt as I threw myself on top of them.

The first guard I took head on, cracking his jaw with a right cross that I threw everything behind. He crumpled to the floor with a whimper.

One of the three guards left felt lucky and swung at my head. I caught the shaft of his baton below the sparking end. I jerked him in close, lowering my head and slamming it into his nose.

He fell under a shower of blood.

The remaining two guards were less eager to rush

in. They circled me, lowering their stances and choosing their attacks.

"Jax, Angel," the man with the deep voice ordered.

"No," Jax said, leaning back in his chair. "No, I'm not fighting my own family."

Angel actually stood up and walked over to me.

I felt confident I could take her in a one-on-one fight, but if she went invisible on me, it would make it that much harder. I wasn't sure how to fight something I couldn't see.

Fists clenched, I followed her movements, ready for anything.

Instead of going invisible or even swinging at me, she leaned down, picking up the two electric batons on the ground and handed them to me.

"Here, it's more of a fair fight now," Angel said, scrunching her brow. "Actually, this was never a fair fight at all. Just finish them and get this over with."

"Insubordination!" the deep-voiced man in the monitor yelled.

"Wesley?" the female founder asked. "You're not going to do anything?"

"I told you after what you did to Amber that I was done if you ever hurt one of them again," Cage said, taking his cigar from the tray and putting it in the corner of his mouth. "You told me if I stayed on, nothing would happen to them. I'm content to let things play out."

The deep-voiced man let out a string of curse words that sounded like poetry. I was actually impressed.

The last two Immortal Corp guards hedged their bets and moved in on me at once.

I ignored the one behind me altogether. I took a giant step toward the man rushing me and lifted my other foot from the ground. My boot made contact with his sternum, cracking it in half as I slammed into him.

He fell to the ground, gasping.

I knew this was going to offer the guard behind me a free shot, but I didn't really care. I needed to feel some pain right now. Maybe it would clear my head. The guard behind me rammed his electric baton into my back.

A hot, sharp stinging sensation sent me stumbling forward.

I fell to the floor in a roll and came up on a single knee. The guard pressed his attack, not anticipating that I would turn my fall into a roll. He thought I was going down.

He rushed me with a baton over his head. I caught him with both of my own batons in his gut. The guy shook and spasmed on his feet as the electric current ran through him. His hair actually stood on end.

After a few seconds, I removed the batons and let him fall to the ground, smoking.

"Order more guards into the room," the man with the deep voice bellowed. "Bring in Number Eight. She'll teach him a lesson."

"Enough," the silent man spoke again. He actually rose from his seat. He was still in shadow, but I could guess he wore some kind of suit jacket. He was tall.

"We're fighting and arguing like a dysfunctional family when the real threat lies six days from now," the silent man said. "If it helps mend wounds and sets your mind on the aliens where it should be, then we'll tell you what we know about Amber. Echo did try to kill her. He would have, but she was rescued by who we believe was the Order."

I dropped my batons on the floor. It had felt great to set some of my aggression loose.

"I don't believe you," I said. "How can I?"

"Then don't," the man said. "Go and see for yourself. There's no body in her grave. The burial was an act. We never found a body."

"Amber's out there, somewhere, alive?" Angel voiced.

"We have to find her," Jax said. "We will find her."

Hope sparked in my heart for the first time since I could remember. A dozen questions had to be pushed back at the same time. Had the Order really saved her? Where was she now? Was she okay? Was she a prisoner of theirs now? That was five years ago. Was she still alive today?

I didn't say another word and instead made my way out of the room.

"There are still important matters to discuss about the invasion," the woman said to my back. "Daniel, you need to—"

"Let him go," the silent man who wasn't so silent anymore stated. "Let him go."

EPILOGUE

WITH X'S DIRECTIONS, I made my way to Elysium. Stealing a vehicle probably wasn't the nicest option, but I needed to quickly get to the cemetery where Amber was buried.

X brought up all the information she could surrounding the events on the bridge the day Echo had tried to kill Amber. Images, news articles, GG reports all of it said a body was found and buried, but there were no images of the body itself.

"She was trying to contact the Order, when Immortal Corp decided to kill her," I said out loud, sifting through the information I did know. "Maybe the Order knew she was a target for her own company and sent someone to look out for her? Maybe that person fished her out of the lake?"

"Maybe," X said. "The changes made to you and the rest of the Pack Protocol could have altered her lung capacity. Perhaps she was able to breathe underwater, or hold her breath longer than normal. Daniel, I don't want you to set yourself up for more heartache if we do in fact find a body in that coffin."

"I know," I said, staring out the window of the stolen vehicle. The sun was just setting as we entered the city of Elysium. It had been a whole lot of nothing between the two cities, but the roadway was new and traffic minimal.

"Where do we draw the line between hope and foolishness?" I asked out loud. I didn't really expect X to have an answer to that one. I was just thinking out loud.

"I think humans need to hope," X said. "Hope is what keeps them alive. Hope for a better tomorrow, for a brighter future."

"You're making too much sense," I said, leaning back in the driver side seat while the self-driving feature took us to our destination. "You would have made a great philosopher."

"Naw," X said, teasing me. "I'd leave that to you. I'm happy with being support."

We rode the rest of the way in silence.

We snaked our way through the streets of Elysium

as night took over. I watched the holo display on the front windshield of the vehicle we stole count down the kilometers to the cemetery.

There was no turning back now. One way or the other, we were going to get some answers. Either Immortal Corp was full of crip and I was going to dig up Amber's dead body or the coffin was empty and there was a possibility she was still out there.

We pulled up to the cemetery grounds an hour later. Full darkness covered the night sky.

Like most people, I wasn't big on cemeteries, especially at night. But unlike most people, I had a grave to rob. I parked the vehicle on the side of the curb. Wrought-iron black gates to the grounds stopped my progress for a moment.

On the front sign of the cemetery was their operating hours as well as their name, "Saint Michelson Cemetery."

"I'm not familiar with that saint," I thought out loud. "Guess it's better that way."

I looked around, making sure we were alone before hopping the fence. There wasn't anyone within eye distance. In a city like this with everything so wide and open the cemetery took up a city block by itself.

I guess I wasn't the only one that didn't want to be in a cemetery at night. Only gentle rolling dirt hills opened up in front of me. Decorative headstones etched from expensive-looking stone lined the pathways.

A single-story building I guessed was the office was located in the middle of the grounds. A shed sat next to it. The light was on in the shed. Probably the maintenance man.

At least that was what I told myself to hinder any macabre thoughts of ghosts conjured in my mind.

"She should be in the upper right hand corner," X told me. "At least that's what I'm getting from how this place is set up."

X gave me directions as I followed the path she set out. There were hundreds of gravestones , all with names I didn't recognize. They all had stories, loved ones probably, and definitely came from money.

Each marker was more prestigious than the next. It was almost as if the dead occupants were competing with one another from beyond the next world.

I followed the path over to the rear right hand side where a series of much smaller headstones were placed. These looked like the classic tombstones I was used to seeing. They were short and stubby, shaped like an arch. I found the alias Amber had been buried under, Jasmine Adams. It was the name X had found for her in the records.

There was no quote or special marker for her, just a name and a date.

I fell to my knees, running my hand over the name as memories flooded my mind.

"I guess I really didn't think this through," I said, looking at the hard ground underneath me. "I should have brought a shovel."

"The shed," X said.

I nodded, getting to my feet and going over. As I approached, I could hear someone shuffling inside. I was pretty sure it was just a single person muttering under his breath.

I peeked my head into the barn-style doors. A middle-aged man in overalls was puttering around his workshop. An assortment of tools hung on the walls, all clean and shining.

"Now where did I put that?" the man asked himself, running a handkerchief over his wet forehead. He wore a hat and short-sleeve shirt.

He turned and looked at me sideways. He blinked a few times, startled.

"Is it really a person I'm seeing now or another spirit?" he asked, trying to get a better look at me in the dull overhead light of his shed. "I told you spirits I have no quarrel with you."

"I'm not a spirit," I said, walking into the room. "I

just need to borrow a shovel."

The man's eyes went wide when he saw the MK II at my hip, the axe and knife on my belt.

"You're him then, I guess." The man rubbed his hands together, half in nervousness, half in excitement. "She said you'd be the hard type."

"Who said?" I asked, peering into the darker corners of the shed. "Who told you I was coming?"

"No need to worry. I'm alone." The man walked to a wall of the shed and picked up a wide shovel. He handed it to me. "This one should do the job. The tall woman in my dream said to wait here for you tonight. That you'd need a shovel."

I didn't know how to respond. I accepted the shovel, thinking of my own dream of the woman that looked human enough but had to be an alien.

"She told me to tell you to stay the course," the grounds man said. "She said you'd know what that means. Do you?"

"Yeah, I think so," I said.

"Just put the ground back when you're done," the groundskeeper said. "And leave the shovel. As far as I'm concerned, you were never here."

"Thanks," I said, turning my back to the man. I hesitated and turned around again. "She say anything else?"

"Just that you've been through a lot and could use a hand," the groundskeeper said with a shrug. "I don't get many visitors in my dreams, but when I do, I make it a rule to follow what they tell me to do. Bad luck otherwise."

"Right, bad luck," I said, leaving the shed.

I made my way back to Amber's plot of ground and started. Anyone who's had to dig a hole using a shovel knows it's not an easy job. Even with my enhanced strength, it was a chore.

Despite the coolness of the night air, I started to sweat. Drops of perspiration fell from my forehead. I dug the blade of the shovel in, over and over again. With each shove of the tool, I thought about what I would do if I found her body. I thought about what I would do if there was in fact no body.

Time passed and I lost myself in the rhythm of the scoop of the shovel, emptying the spade and then doing it over and over again.

I wasn't sure how much time passed, but a few meters down, I felt the shovel hit something hard. My hands burned, but my healing factor would deal with that in no time flat.

I cleared off the lid of the coffin. The lid was thick and in two parts. From the middle up, it opened and the bottom portion did the same. The coffin itself was grey. Again, nothing adorned the lid, no name or even a symbol.

I cleaned off the sand and dirt around it to be able to open the upper half of the coffin.

"You ready for this?" I asked X, tossing the shovel to the side. I stood on top of the lower half of the coffin, looking down at the upper section.

"Are you?" X asked.

"As ready as I'm ever going to be," I said.

I grabbed the edge of the top of the coffin and forced it up. A wall of dirt and sand fell into the open coffin as I lifted the lid. I leaned back, looking inside.

I didn't have a lot of light to work with. The dual moons overhead and the stars shone down. There were a few lights in the cemetery, but deep into the ground, they weren't of much use.

I looked into the darkness of the coffin.

It wasn't empty.

Not a body, but a piece of clothing I recognized rested in the casket, a black mask with a modified red cross on it. There was a horizontal line like the traditional symbol and smaller horizontal line below it.

I'd seen the emblem before. It belonged to the Order.

Start Reading Vendetta book 4 in the Forsaken Mercenary Universe, today!

STAY INFORMED

Get A Free Book by visiting Jonathan Yanez' website. You can email me at jonathan.alan.yanez@gmail.com or find me on Amazon, and Instagram (@author_jonathan_yanez). I also created a special Facebook group called "Jonathan's Reading Wolves" specifically for readers, where I show new cover art, do giveaways, and run contests. Please check it out and join whenever you get the chance!

For updates about new releases, as well as exclusive promotions, visit my website and sign up for the VIP mailing list. Head there now to receive free stories.

www.jonathan-yanez.com

Enjoying the series? Help others discover *Forsaken Mercenary* by sharing with a friend.

BOOKS IN THE FORSAKEN MERCENARY UNIVERSE

2. Cassie

Made in United States
Troutdale, OR
08/22/2023

12285576R00200